Travis Cooper Bounty Hunter

a collection of 9 Travis Cooper Tales

Lewis Kirts

A Warthog Press Publication
rev. 7.6.2023

Printed in the United States of America

* * *

This is a work of fiction. Names, characters, places, and incidents are either the product of the author's imagination or used fictitiously. Any resemblance to actual events, locales, organizations or persons, living or dead, is entirely coincidental and beyond the intent of the author and publisher.

Cover design & interior format by Debora Lewis
deboraklewis@yahoo.com

Photo courtesy of Shutterstock.com

ISBN: 9798376718926

Pertinent Information about Me

The *k* is silent in words such as knee, know, knot and knife. Nobody seems to have a problem with that. So why do they want to knock me upside the head when I tell them the *r* in wash is invisible?

To Kartchner Ventures LLC,
and all the hard-working volunteers at Mescal Movie Set.
Thank you for bringing life back to the old west.

A special thanks to Tom Kimmel — one of the many Mescal volunteers — for his input and insight into Travis Cooper.

Contents

The Clear Blue of it All

A Travis Cooper Tale

Mama, all five-foot-one of her, feigned indifference when, once again, Papa, her husband of eighteen years, informed her he had to go north for a few weeks to help at the stockyards up near Fort Grant.

With both hands on hips, Papa took his stance. "Now, Millie, you know it's the only job out there. We need the income and this is the best way I can figure to provide. I'll bring home a beef and a few coins. I always do, don't I?" Papa peered over at me, then back to Mama. "I think Travis should take a week off of church-goin' and help me again this time out."

Mama huffed, stirred the stew she was cooking, then pointed the soup ladle at him. "And who is gonna help me out around here? I need Travis here to tend the mule and get me to church. He's missed enough of his Bible lessons as it is." She commenced to stirring while shaking a finger at him. "That boy needs his learnin', and the best way to get it is through the word of our Lord."

Papa pointed toward the north. "He's closer to God out yonder – under the clear blue of it all – than he is in that damn church of yours!"

"That's it, Miles! Go! But you're not taking Travis with you." She threw the soup ladle into the dishpan. "There's jobs right here in Pomerene. I don't see why you have to go north. I think you just go to avoid gettin' a good Christian education."

I pushed my bowl away, glanced at Mama, then spoke to Papa. "I know enough about your line of work, and while I want to help with providing, I think Mama needs a little help with gettin' the garden planted before the heat sets in, and for hitchin' the wagon for church."

Mama smiled at me, then turned to Papa. "He stays here this time."

More than two weeks passed with no word from Papa, and I wondered if he'd turned bad for good. I'd been with him a time or two, for his *job*, and I didn't think his way of life was what I wanted for myself. I figured there must be a better way to take care of Mama, and when we got word of Papa's untimely death, I knew what task lay ahead. I aimed to make a living at setting things straight for Mama, and for anyone else who'd lost a loved one, a fortune — or even two bits — to anyone dealing from the bottom.

My first task was to sell our small spread, move Mama into Benson, and get me a good horse and outfit. A few more dollars spent, and I had me an old, but reliable, revolver. What I needed now was backup.

Like I said, I'd ridden with Papa on a few occasions, and while he'd taught me a bit about his line of work and how to read people, I wasn't sure about the other side of things, and how to go about dealing with the law.

I thought on it and decided to put it all on the line and find someone I thought might hear me out, and back me up.

I made sure Mama had food, a few extra dollars, and a warm room in the boarding house, then I hit the road for Bisbee — the headquarters of the Arizona Rangers. I figured that might be a good place to start.

Just two miles south of Benson, I ran into a group of Arizona Rangers. Their captain, a man by the name of Fitzsimmons, heard me out.

Fitzsimmons shook his head. "I don't know, kid. I think you should leave this to Sheriff McLeod. Come on to Benson with us and I'll help you make your case."

I shook my head and looked at the ground. "Can't do that, sir." I sighed and looked him in the eye. "I have to settle this myself so I can get on with things."

Fitzsimmons worked at talking me out of my plan, but when he realized I wasn't gonna heed his warnings, he offered his hand.

I accepted, we shook, and he gave me the information I'd need to get him behind me once I figured out who was behind Papa's demise.

At fifteen, still way shy of sixteen, I now had a line on a new way to provide for Mama. I just had to prove myself.

I found a job on a ranch just outside of Benson. An honest outfit with honest work. Twenty and found would provide what I needed and would put money in the bank for Mama. Two months in, and I got a day off to visit her. She was happier than I'd seen her in a while, and I think a warm bed, three squares and a roof that didn't leak — even during monsoons — was the cause. Not to mention a church just down the street. But I sensed her gay mood was more for my benefit than reality.

I got a few dollars out of the bank, took her shopping, and then to supper in her brand-new dress. I think it might have been the first dress she hadn't made, or at least repaired from a hand-me-down she'd received through the church.

Mama finished her meal, politely put her cloth napkin on her empty plate, sat up straight and looked me in the eye. "I'm trustin' you, Travis. I was never sure about your papa and his jobs, and maybe I'll never know the truth about his death, or if that was really him they buried, but I hope I've taught you well— me and the Lord, that is." She leaned back, sighed and looked down at the plain gold band Papa had placed on her hand all those years ago. "I loved that man. I truly did. I just wish life was a bit easier for him. I'm glad you left word at the old place, just in case they hear anything more about what happened to him, and I hope he taught you a bit about life and how to get along in this world, before he left it. I think the Lord provides for all — but four-fold for those who try to provide for themselves."

I reached for Mama's hand. "I've been providin', and I'll continue. And I promise you this: If I get word about Papa's death, I'll make sure any wrongdoing against him will be dealt with. So, if you don't hear from me for a bit, don't worry. Money — *honest money* — will be put into your account as best I can. I'll visit when possible, and send postcards often. If you need anything, you get word to me. I hear the sheriff here in Benson is a good man, so let him know and tell him where I work. He'll get word to the ramrod and I'll come runnin'. I love you, Mama, but I gotta head back. Let me walk you to the boarding house."

Mama seemed a bit frail for her age, and I wondered if it was because she missed Papa. With Mama settled in her room, I took leave. On the way out, I spoke with Mrs. Riches, the owner of the boarding house. "Here's an extra bit of money. Please make sure Mama has anything she needs. She gets chilled easy, so an extra blanket might help. Get word to me of any of her needs. She's not likely to complain or ask for anything."

She put her hand on my arm. "You're a good son. I hope you're a good man. I've heard rumors about your papa. Seems he was in a bad bunch and paid the price."

She had piqued my interest. "What did you hear... and where?"

"I was in the mercantile and overheard a rancher from Dragoon talking about a gang your papa had ridden with. Miles Cooper, right?"

I nodded and she proceeded to tell me what she'd overheard regarding a man by the name of Jed Bigler. I listened. I planned. I figured to send a postcard to Bisbee to see if that ranger, Fitzsimmons, would back me.

I thanked Mrs. Riches for the information, tipped my hat and started for the door. She grabbed my arm again.

"Travis — your mother puts on a good show, but from time to time, I hear her crying. She's hurting, and I don't think there is a thing in this world that will help her get over the loss of your papa." She let go of my arm. Her expression sorrowful. "I just thought you should know."

I left with an uneasy feeling about Mama. I just hoped she would overcome her grief and enjoy life, if just a bit. And I hoped she would understand that justice had been done once I'd taken care of those who'd murdered Papa. Maybe, then, anguish would be replaced with joy.

I got a postcard and addressed it to Captain Robert Fitzsimmon in Bisbee, outlining my plan. I had a good idea of where to find this Jed Bigler. When you work as a ranch hand, you hear stories about rustlers, their tactics and their hunting ground, and that name had come up a time or two. From what I gathered, there were four in that bunch, and all of them were said to be ruthless.

Impatience, being a fault of mine, might have gotten the better of me if it were not for Sheriff Joe McLeod. I'd spoken with him about my plans and he urged me to wait for the rangers. As much as I wanted justice for my father, I knew McLeod was right and I'd have to bide my time.

I booked a room in the hotel and had a meal at Café Bonita. I tried, but couldn't sleep, so at four in the morning, gave up. I headed down to the hotel lobby, procured a table in the dining area, and ordered buttermilk biscuits and sausage gravy.

Just as I was taking my first bite, Captain Fitzsimmons pulled up a chair and joined me.

We ate in relative silence — but he was watching me. I think he was sizing me up — trying to decide if I was fit for the task.

Plates cleared and coffee refilled, Fitzsimmons sat back. He eyed me for a moment. "You sure about this, kid?"

I leaned back. I was relaxed and confident about what I was planning to do. "I'm sure."

"I've got three men with me. We'll back you as long as we think you've got this figured right. If we think this isn't working the way you planned, we'll step in and get you out of there. Sound fair?"

"Just don't give up on me. Stay back and I'll signal when I'm ready for you to bring down the wrath of God on them. I might be able to take one, but the other three are all yours."

Fitzsimmons stood. "I'll introduce you. Wouldn't want one of my men thinking you're one of them. Follow me."

Introductions were made, concerns voiced — and dealt with.

I was heading out, and hoping that everything Mama, *and Papa*, had taught me would help me while I was under the clear blue of it all.

Lessons

A Travis Cooper Tale

I had a different education than most. Papa taught me the particulars of profitable cattle rustling. Problem was, Papa lost a whole lot more than he ever made. But every cloud, well, let's just say that what I learned from Papa saved my ass time and time again, and helped me sort out some of the mysteries of life.

Mama never knew about Papa's line of work until his forced retirement. Trusting to a fault, she assumed the money and beef he acquired was from honest work at the stockyard up near Fort Grant in the Arizona Territory. I can't say Papa ever really lied to her, but he never told her the whole truth, and if anyone could have made an honest man out of him, it was Mama with her Bible lessons.

Papa lived in two worlds, and I saw the humor and the tragedy of both, so when I decided to diversify the family business, Mama had all the information she needed now, but no matter how hard she tried, Mama didn't think she could ever make an honest man out of me.

"'Scuse me."

Three plates fell to the ground and three pistols came up.

I dropped my saddle and put my hands in the air. "Don't s'pose you got an extra plate of beans and maybe a cup of coffee that ain't been claimed yet?"

Two of the guns disappeared into holsters as two men reclaimed their seats, while the third went right on pointing his gun in my direction, and the man who held that gun worked to get control of a twitch in his left eye. He kicked his plate aside, then took a step forward and growled, "How the hell'd you sneak by Del?" He glanced down the path that led to the meadow. "Del, how the hell'd he sneak by you!"

My hands still high, I said, "He was relievin' himself, so I skipped the pleasantries and came on in. Shucks. Didn't mean to cause a ruckus. Just hungry and thirsty, is all." I glanced toward the pot on the fire.

He scratched just beneath the twitch. "Del! Get in here!"

Del wandered in. "What, Boss?"

It took him a moment, but when he finally noticed me, he looked me up and down, balled one hand into a fist and worked it hard against the open palm of the other. "Who the hell are you?"

At about six foot six and pushing three hundred pounds of gristle, I knew that Del was the kind of man you sent in to do the heavy stuff. The kind of man who can get the job done when nothing but fists and feet will do, when the brains of the operation ran out of alternatives, or maybe just needed a bit of entertainment on a slow day.

"Travis Cooper. Pleasure, Del."

Del glanced at the boss, then for lack of any better response, stuck out his hand. "Pleasure."

The boss had been trying to figure me and was coming up blank. He scratched his cheek, then offered his hand. "Jed Bigler."

The two by the fire took the introduction as a signal to return to their supper. The one on the right picked up his plate, snorted and spit, and the one on the left ground his right boot toe into the dirt sending up a small puff of dust that was lost in the draft of the flames, while Del wheezed out an idiot's chuckle and moseyed on back to his post beyond the firelight. I had them figured and that was lesson two, courtesy of Papa. Now, to work on lesson three. Act young and dumb. And lie if you have to.

"Got mixed up with a little girl down around Elfrida." I rubbed my hands against my hips as if they were sweaty. "Shucks. Didn't know her to be married, else I wouldn't have bedded her. Figgered to make myself scarce, but I left in such a hurry that I didn't bring no food. Been a two-day ride on nothin' but water." I looked toward the pot on the fire and licked my lips.

Bigler laughed, the twitch in his left eye all but gone. "Leroy, throw him a plate. He's lookin' a little lean, and as sneaky as he is, I might just find a way for him to pay off his food."

"I sure don't mind workin' for my supper. Just wish I could figger a way to make enough to send a little somethin' to Mama." I continued with the lie I'd rehearsed. "I've been takin' care of her since Papa took off with her sister. Nobody'd hire me for honest wages, so I took to thievin' chickens and hooked up on a rustle or two to make ends meet. Guess that's where the sneaky comes in. Mama don't know. She wouldn't stand for thievin', but women need took care of and that was all I could think to do. I left her a note sayin' I'd gone huntin' work up north. She'll be expectin' to hear from me inside of a month, I s'pose." I rubbed my hands on my hips, then looked toward Leroy. He snorted and spit, then pitched a plate and I let it fall through my hands, then juggled the fork that followed. I settled the fork in my left pocket, then scrambled to pick up the plate. I grabbed at the hot ladle, then pulled back and shook my hand as if I'd been burned.

Bigler's twitch no longer tormented him as he took my plate, filled it with beans, then carefully placed a couple of corn dodgers alongside them. A little sentiment came out with the gruff. "Eat up, boy. I think I can make use of you."

I settled down on my saddle and worked myself right into lesson number four. *Act trusting and trustworthy.* I stuck a finger in my beans, then pulled it out and licked it. "Thanks, plenty, Mr. Bigler."

"How old are you, boy?"

I shoveled in three forkfuls, and with half of them still in my mouth, I slurped to keep them from running down my chin. "Fifteen."

His twitch started up again.

I swallowed hard. "Well, in about seven months, that is."

"Kind'a big for fourteen."

"I guess my size is what got Luanne all riled up. She figgered me to be sixteen, and when she got to workin' on me I couldn't stop. Never done that before." I snorted a little and grinned. "Wouldn't mind tryin' it again, though." I stared at the fire for another moment with that grin on my face, then with wide eyes, looked up. "Oh, no, Mr. Bigler! Hope you don't think I'd lie to you 'bout nothin'! Just figgered addin' a couple months to my age don't make all that much difference."

His twitch lessened just a little. "You'd best not lie to me, boy, or you won't be needin' no supper!"

Eyes still wide, I said, "Oh, no, Mr. Bigler, Sir! Sometimes you gotta thieve to eat, but I can't think of one good reason for lyin'!" I kept that honest look on my face until his twitch was gone, then turned and eyed the pot of beans again.

"Go on, boy. Eat up. Almost a full moon t'night. We'll see if you can hold on."

"Thanks, plenty, Mr. Bigler." I ladled up some beans and grabbed two more dodgers out of the sack by the fire, and nodded as I sat back down. "Thanks, plenty."

Bigler walked out of camp the same direction I'd come in. I supposed he wanted to see what I'd ridden in on and maybe take care of some personal matters while Leroy and the other fellow had a little bit of time with me. I finished my beans and pushed on to lesson number five. *Ask for acceptance.* Setting my plate on the ground I stood up and rubbed my hands on my hips. "Hope you fella's don't mind me eatin' your grub." Leroy spit and the other fellow worked his right boot against the ground. "You tell me how, and I'll get these plates cleaned up and stowed. That's a right fancy holster you got there, Mr. Leroy. You was quick to draw when I come in. I never shot a pistol but a couple a times before Papa run out on us. Maybe if Mr. Bigler lets me help out, you could show me how to shoot. Got an old one in my bags. No bullets through." I turned to the other fellow. "You was quick, too. Maybe 'tween the two of you I could learn a little somethin', you know, just enough to even things out if we come up on a bunch that don't like us." I looked down at the ground. "That's if Mr. Bigler keeps me on. Sure would help a lot, havin' a little somethin' to send to Mama."

Leroy chuckled and punched the other fellow in the arm. "Damn, Johnny. Looks like we got us a boy to help out around here."

I looked up and nodded. "You fella's just tell me what to do, and I'll do my best to make you proud." I looked back down. "Hope Mr. Del don't have a problem with me. Shucks. Didn't mean to get Mr. Bigler riled at him. Just didn't wanna interrupt while he was taken care of business out there and them beans smelled too good to wait it out."

Johnny laughed. "Del ain't got enough sense to have a problem."

Leroy snorted and spit as he glared at Johnny.

Johnny rubbed his right toe in the dirt, then took a deep breath and puffed out his chest. "Grab them plates, Trav. We gotta get cleaned up and get some shuteye before we head out."

I rubbed my hands on my hips. "Yes, sir, Mr. Johnny!" I did as I was told and had them laughing at my ineptness for such things as wiping out plates and squelching a fire, without as much as one snort and spit from Leroy, or a boot toe rubbing the dirt from Johnny. When Mr. Bigler came back, I was ready for lesson six. *Praise them and gain friendship.*

I looked Bigler in the eye, rubbed my hands on my hips and nodded toward the horses. "Left a tin of hard candy in my bags. Kind'a like somethin' sweet before I turn in, and need to take care of business anyways." His eye started twitching and I said, "Just wanna be honest and tell you I got a gun out there, too. No bullets."

"Go on, boy. But you let Del know what you're up to. Don't have no time for funerals."

"Yes, Sir."

I stopped just shy of the open range and watched Del for a moment. With his arms across his chest and his rifle a good five feet away, he sat stock-still on an outcropping of boulders that looked out over acres of Arizona ranch land that didn't seem to have a beginning or an end, but I was pretty sure it had an owner. I grabbed a fallen limb from one of the mesquites and broke it over my knee. Del jumped up as if a scorpion had gotten hold of the smarter end of him, then he went for his rifle. I gave him the time he needed, then with arms high, I stepped onto the range. "Just me, Mr. Del. Travis."

Del's sigh of relief brought out a wheeze from his lungs and a stream of snot from his nose. As he rolled a piece of candy from his tongue to his jaw, he rested his rifle against the boulders, grabbed a kerchief from his back pocket, blew his nose, then checked the kerchief for content.

I slowly lowered my arms. "Just came out for some hard candy and to do my business. Mr. Bigler said to check in with you. Guess you must be his right-hand man. That's a big responsibility. He must put a lot of stock in you and I can see why. Don't believe I ever seen a man heft a rifle that quick. You'd be hard to beat, but in a smart outfit like this, I doubt you have to use it all that much 'cept maybe for some supper meat."

Del grinned with all but three side teeth intact. He moved the candy around and it clinked on his teeth as he pushed it back to his jaw. "Had to use it a few times. Don't need it for close work."

"I knew a man a while back in Elfrida that was good with a rifle. He was one of them that could hit what he aimed for, all the while knowin' it needed to be hit. He could read a man from a mile away. You got that same look about you, Mr. Del."

Still grinning Del moved the candy to the front and held it between his teeth for me to see, then stuck it to the side again. "Hope you don't mind. I was hangin' your bags on the tree and found your candy."

"Not at all, Mr. Del. I was fixin' on askin' did you want some or not. You want another piece?"

"Wouldn't mind one in my pocket for later."

"You comin' in for some shut eye?"

"Nope, slept all mornin'. I'll ride when they ride, then catch a little sleep after."

"This seems like a right good spot with that grove of trees for cover and the river for water. A smart man picked this spot. Did you pick it, Mr. Del?"

"My brother picked it. I woulda chose the one up the river a ways."

"I rode through there. That woulda been my choice, too. Who's your brother?"

"Jed."

I told him the same story I'd told the others, then embellished just a little more. "Had me a little brother, but Papa took him along. I was always takin' the blame and he was always gettin' the credit, so I'm better off without him around. Maybe by now Papa realizes that I was the one who carried the weight." I looked down and kick up a little dirt. "Shucks, Mr. Del. Didn't mean to get you in trouble with your little brother. Come on over and get some of that candy whenever you want. I'd better finish up and get back so he don't come lookin' for me."

Del put one arm on my shoulder as we walked. "Nobody'll bother you while I'm around, Trav."

I left Del at the boulders with two pieces of hard candy in his pocket, then headed back to camp to do some thinking, and lying on my back looking through the fluttering mesquite leaves at the sky above seemed like a good place to do it. As soon as I entered camp I stretched one hand above my head, the other out to the side, yawned and breathed a sigh of exhaustion.

Bigler took a swig out of a bottle, then growled, "You'd better turn in, boy." He corked the bottle and wiped his mouth on his shirtsleeve. "Leroy, Johnny, you too."

Leroy spit and Johnny ground his foot in the dirt, but both did as they were told while Bigler scratched under that twitch. The moon rose over the Rincons and Bigler paced while I thought. *Leroy is the fastest with a pistol, Johnny has a mouth that can cause trouble, and Bigler thinks he's in charge. And maybe he's supposed to be, but he recognizes resentment and suspects trouble from within. Now, Del, well, I have to hear a little more, but right now I'm thinking he'd rather be out chasing butterflies. The problem with a man like Del? Whether he pulls off their wings.*

Bigler stood over me. "Why aren't you sleepin' yet, boy?"

"I'm tuckered out, that's for sure. Just not use to sleepin' outside, I s'pose." I yawned and rolled to my side. He stood there for a moment, then went on to other chores as I hashed over the last couple of months.

Since I'd been on my own, this was the third outfit I'd come across that had potential. I had to wonder if the hierarchy of this bunch had recently changed. It seemed that Bigler struggled for control, and Del might very well be the only reason he had it. There were six horses not including mine, and I didn't see where they had cause for those two extra, and even so, the extra saddle and gear looked familiar. It could have pointed to losing a man, getting shed of one, *or eliminating a rival.*

A few minutes alone with Johnny will provide me with answers, but for now, I'll sleep on what I know.

Someone kicked the bottom of my boot and I woke with a start. Del wheezed out a laugh. "Jed says to get you up and mounted." He handed me my pistol. "It's loaded so don't be pointin' it at nobody. Jed argued the point, but I stood for you and told him you best not go out without it."

I wiped a little slobber from my face, stood up and looked at Del with feigned astonishment. "Shucks, Del. Don't know what to say. I'll be extra careful and make you proud of me." I slowly rolled the cylinder knowing anything in it would be blanks, then smiled up at Del. "I got six bullets. I'll pay you back just as soon as I'm able."

"If you gotta use it, just point and pull. You might get close enough to scare 'em."

"Thanks, Del." *Papa's lessons are paying off.*

We rode about an hour and just as the moon was at its apex and the Dragoons towered above us, Jed put up his hand. "Leroy, come with me. The rest of you stay put."

Del moved up to get a better view. I leaned toward Johnny and whispered, "What are we stoppin' for, Mr. Johnny?"

"There's a corral over yonder. They've been movin' in stolen horses to take north. We figure to save them the trip. Run across one of their men a while back. He told us a good bit while he was able." He chuckled. "Del, didn't much like him, but Jed likes his horse."

"What did Del do to him?"

"Poked out his eyes, took his boots and sent him runnin'. Ran across him the next day, but there wasn't much left to worry with so we left him wanderin' against the elements. Ain't the first, won't be the last. Best stay straight with Del."

Del pulls off the wings. I squirmed and leather creaked as I settled back in. "Are we takin' these horses tonight?"

"Naw. Just checkin' on 'em. Won't have 'em all here for a couple more days." As Del rode toward us, Johnny whispered, "You best stay straight."

Del stopped right next to me and I shivered. He broke into a grin. "Hey, Trav. Got any of that hard candy with you?

I glanced at Johnny, then smiled. "Sure do, Mr. Del. You want a piece?"

"Got a hankerin'."

I had a lot to think about on the ride back. I'd watched these men for two days before I walked in on them, and the four men who had come with me didn't think I stood a chance, but they didn't know how much Papa had taught me before he was *forced into retirement.* I hoped like hell they hadn't written me off and were still at that other little grove of mesquites just up the river, but I wouldn't know for sure until first light. I had two lessons left up my sleeve, but the rest I'd have to make up as I went along.

I fell back and Del waited up. He poked me with his rifle and the hard candy clinked against his teeth. "Kinda quiet there, Trav."

I yawned. "Just tired is all, Mr. Del."

"We get these horses north and paid for, I'll get you some more hard candy."

I played scared as I glanced around. "You think... you think there'll be... any... any shootin'?"

"Nope."

"Why's that?"

He patted his rifle that lay across his lap and wheezed out a laugh. "I'll clean 'em out before you go in."

"Shucks, Mr. Del. I sure would be worried about havin' to shoot a man. Don't think I could ever look Mama in the eye again without her seein' through me."

He rolled the candy around in his mouth. "It don't matter if you gotta kill one of 'em." He paused, then chuckled. "They ain't nobody."

I poured Johnny the last of the coffee, started another pot, then rubbed my hands on my hips. "Sun's comin' up. Del said for me to wake him."

Bigler growled. "Best wait 'til that coffee is ready."

"Yes, Sir, Mr. Bigler."

A few minutes later, a little bit of coffee perked out and sizzled in the hot coals. I looked at Bigler and he nodded. Cautiously, I nudged Del's left foot with my boot. He wheezed and snorted, then sat up and laughed. "Learn anything last night, Trav?"

"Sure did, Mr. Del." I grabbed my pistol from my waistband and Del never flinched. "I learned I sure would feel better if you taught me how to use this thing." Smiling, I looked around. Bigler's eye wasn't twitching and Johnny wasn't grinding his toe in the dirt. *Lesson number seven almost complete. Test for trust.*

Del stood, wheezed and chuckled, then took my pistol from me and stuck it back in my waistband. "Need a cup and a smoke first." He looked at Bigler. "Takin' him out with me today."

"First thing you'd better teach him is where to point that thing." Bigler's eye twitched and he jabbed Del in the chest with his finger. "No shootin'. Don't need any attention this way."

Del put his hand on my shoulder. He had a bit of resentment in his voice. "Won't let him pull the trigger, Boss."

I knew he wanted to protect me, and I smiled up at him. "Thanks, Mr. Del. Just show me how to aim."

Bigler growled. "Grab some grub, get your coffee and take him with you."

While Del got his coffee, I made a few bacon biscuits for him and we headed out to relieve Leroy of watch.

"Shucks, Mr. Del. Don't know the last time I had this much fun... well... 'cept maybe with that girl down in Elfrida." I pulled my pistol and aimed at a passing bird. "Pow!" I laughed. "Think I got that one?"

"You're gettin' a little faster, but I doubt you woulda hit 'im. You're stoppin' when you ought'a follow through."

I shoved the gun back in my waistband. "Want some hard candy?"

Del grinned. "Hopin' you'd ask."

"I'll get some."

I reached in my bags and pulled out my tin of hard candy, took the top off and shoved it in my pocket along with a couple pieces of candy and wandered back to Del. "Here's a piece. Gotta go take care of business."

Del popped the candy in his mouth and grinned, then turned his back to me like I knew he would. I walked out a ways, squatted down, took the blanks out of my pistol and replace them with six cartridges from a pouch on the inside of my boot. I took the lid from my tin and rubbed it against my shirt to bring out a little bit of a shine, then flashed five short bursts of sunlight toward the other little grove of trees. I went back to Del and waited.

Five minutes passed before a ruckus back at camp got Del's attention. I stepped to the side, just a little ahead, and watched him. He grabbed his rifle and stood facing the path leading in just as four Arizona Rangers, headed by Captain Robert Fitzsimmons, escorted Bigler, Johnny and Leroy into the meadow. Del wheezed when he hefted his rifle to his shoulder, aimed at the ranger in front, and grinned. One shot was all it took. Del hit the ground, his left eye missing along with the back of his head. A piece of hard candy rolled out of his mouth, I scratched my cheek, snorted and spit, then ground the candy into the dirt with the toe of my boot. "An eye for an eye. Lesson number one..." I shoved my pistol in my waistband. "...courtesy of Mama."

If I'd been with Papa that day, maybe it wouldn't have come to this, but Mama insisted I take her to church and maybe learn a few things while I was at it. A rancher, down around Dragoon, found Papa wandering half blind, his left eye dangling on his cheek. Bootless and dying of thirst, he was dead before they got him home, and Mama died soon after, from missing him. That was seven months ago, just shy of my sixteenth birthday, and just one week later I took up bounty hunting.

Papa might have ventured to the wrong side of the law, but he never killed anybody, and he *was* somebody to Mama and me. Among other things, Del was dead wrong about that.

Teach a Boy to Fish

A Travis Cooper Tale

Mama's passing had me out of sorts for a bit, but I knew she'd want me to make use of the lessons she'd taught me.

I'd kept in touch with Robert Fitzsimmons, the Arizona Ranger who had helped me rid the world of the gang who had murdered Papa, and he called on me a few times when a bounty hunter had more of a chance than a man with a badge.

That's what I had become. A bounty hunter. No badge. Just a need for retribution or justice — whichever the face on the handbill deserved.

A little shy on years, tall and lanky for build, and sure I was full up on the lessons of life — taught or experienced — I set out on my first solo hunt. I tracked the man for five days just north of Gleeson. Watched him and thought I had a clear path for getting that bounty. I soon found out I hadn't learned enough. The hunted had clobbered me from behind and now I was in his grip.

I looked up through the hole in the roof at the bright blue of the Arizona sky, then batted my eyes like the sun was half blinding me. I closed my eyes. After several minutes I bobbed my head a bit so my captive would think I'd fallen asleep, or passed out from the blow he'd landed on my head. Once I remained still, I snorted a bit so he'd think I was out cold, snoring. That gave me time for uninterrupted thinking.

Several plans came to mind, but for one reason or another, all were soon eliminated. I guess all that tracking and thinking tired me right out, 'cause next thing you know, I was looking through that hole in the roof and seeing the moon where the sun had previously been.

My captor, an outlaw I knew by the name of Cornwall Norris, was smiling as he turned up the coal oil lamp that hung just above my head. "I see you're awake."

I didn't like his smile. I didn't like this stable. I didn't like the fact that my gun was gone. I didn't like my situation, but I'd caused it, and now I'd have to be the one to fix it. And then it hit me.

Maybe I'd have to work my way back to the wrong side of the law to get this job done. I'd played the wrong side before. I'd played it when I'd brought vengeance down on Papa's killers. That time I'd started out like I was dumb and worked my way in. But now, sitting, tied to a rough-hewn post in this otherwise empty stable, I'd have to figure a smart way out of the mess I'd gotten myself into. I'd been way too cocky and hadn't figured anyone else had all the learning I'd had. I hadn't watched my back. And now my back was against the proverbial wall.

I looked up at Norris and shook my head as if to get the last of my sleep out in the open. I tilted my head to the side and squinted a bit. "So, just what is it you want of me?"

Norris chortled. "I don't want you at all. You're trespassin' on my territory and hinderin' my plans, but I figured if you were snoopin' around, then you must be up to no good when it comes to *my* well bein'."

"I was just lookin' for a dry place to lay my head. Thought it was comin' on to a storm, what with that wind blowin' up a gale."

"What's your name, boy?"

"I'd tell you it was Billy the Kid, but I doubt it would do a bit of good. Even Billy couldn't talk himself outta this if you had 'cause to do him harm... or to take him in." I tilted my head and pretended to be thinking. "Now, wait a damn minute. Are you a bounty hunter? Are you out for a whale and got a little fish instead?" I laughed. "Who are you really after? Maybe I can help."

Norris scratched his chin and echoed my laughter. "Are you tryin' to tell me you got a price on your head? I doubt you're old enough to have caused enough trouble to be worth the effort of takin' you in. And you think you can help me after I come up on you so easy? I'd do best to let you be on your way... as long as you don't think you can tag along and ruin my day."

I pretended to be offended. "You just surprised me, is all, and I've done plenty to put the law on my tail. And just who are you? Somebody that collects a bounty or somebody who has dollar signs all over his face on a poster?"

"I got more dollar signs on my poster than you'll ever live to see."

"Are you tryin' to tell me this is the end of the line?"

Norris pulled his gun from his holster and put it against my head.

I closed my eyes and said, "If you gotta do it, do it fast. If not, untie me so I can get out of this wet spot I just made."

Again, Norris laughed. He holstered his pistol and reached for his knife. I flinched when he flashed it in my face, but from what I knew of Norris, he'd never killed a man in cold blood and I doubted he'd start with a dumb kid. Norris had no way of knowing who I was or that I knew, all too well, who he was. That's what had come to me after my accidental nap. "Well? Are you gonna kill me or let me relieve myself of what I'm not already sittin' in?"

"I'm gonna cut you loose and then you'd better skedaddle on outta here. I never wanna see you around here again. By accident or on purpose. If you don't know the name Cornwall Norris, you'd be best to study on it and stay clear of me from here on out."

I knew he was just a petty road agent, but I wanted to let on I'd heard him to be more. Wide-eyed, I gasped. "Why, yes sir, Mr. Norris. I didn't know this was your hideout. You won't never catch me around here again." I put my hand in the air. "I swear!"

With that, he cut the rope that held me fast. I rubbed my wrists and my hands to restore feeling. "Can I get up, Sir?"

He shook his knife at me. "Get up and get the hell outta here."

I stumbled as I rose, grasped the post to keep me righted, then ran like hell.

Norris had my horse out back, still saddled. I checked by bags. My gun belt and revolver were there, but I didn't put them on, just yet. I jumped on my horse and hightailed it in the direction I had come. I glanced back. Norris watched as I rode. I stopped once, on purpose, just on the ridge to the west. I looked both ways like I didn't know where I was or where I should go. I glanced back. Norris was still watching. I chose west, toward the Dragoons and the middle of nowhere. I didn't want him to think I could get to any kinda town in a hurry, where I might run my mouth about who'd I'd come across.

Once I was out of sight, I stopped and checked my revolver. Norris had taken my cartridges, just as I had suspected. I dismounted, reached way down into my saddlebag. I removed a bit of leather that I use to cover what I prefer no one find. Under it was my tin of hard candy, a box of cartridges, along with my corn dodgers and a bit of jerky.

Several miles of dust now covered my face. The sun had risen over the Chiricahua mountains about two hours past and I stopped and watched the moon set, now barely visible though the light of day. Just before the pass over the Dragoons, I stopped at a creek to get a bit of good water for my horse, my face, and my parched throat. I'd find a place to rest, then head back toward my bounty in the morning. A bit more educated.

Laid out under an alligator juniper, I thought about my short captivity. While the stall where I'd been held was mostly empty of anything useful, Norris had a pile of supplies out back where he'd tied my horse. The quick look I'd gotten of them told me he wasn't going anywhere any time soon. At least not for long. And if I had my way, he wouldn't be needing any supplies at all. Yuma would provide.

A bit of rest, more water, a corn dodger or two, and just as the sun finally decided to provide warmth and light, I was well on my way back to Norris's hideout. It can get downright cold out here in the desert. Even during monsoons. It might top out at well over one hundred, but at times, it can plunge to a bone-chilling forty once the sun is done with the summer sky. I tend to be up and moving before sunrise, because that first bit of heat way up there in the sky will drive the cold air down and drop the temperature even more, temping me to stay snug in my bedroll. I didn't have time for such comfort. I wrapped my coat tighter and rode on toward my first solo bounty.

I stopped just shy of the ridge where, the previous morning, I had contemplated my direction of departure. I tied my horse to a shrub oak and belly-crawled until I was behind a boulder that rested just below the rise on Norris's side of that ridge. I felt for my gun at my side. Checked to make sure it was fully loaded. Reassurance. I pushed my hat up on my brow and watched for any movement around my recent place of captivity. An hour passed before I spied Norris. He came out and began sorting his supplies. Or maybe looking for something in particular.

Several times, Norris glanced in my direction. I began to wonder if he was expecting me. And then I had a thought. Maybe he's expecting company. Wanted or unwanted? I had to wonder.

I knew he sometimes worked with the gang known at the Dailys. There were three of them, and they weren't known to be as polite as Norris. If they had been there on my previous visit, I doubt I'd still be breathing.

Still on my belly, I backed down the hill, retrieved my horse and headed north. I figured to make circuitous route and come up on Norris from the south. I'd have cover and could watch and sort this out.

When I finally made my way around and came up from the south, the Dailys were indeed present. I watched for about five minutes and deduced that the conversation that was taking place was heated, to say the least.

Four to one aren't the best odds. I'd be here a while if I wanted just Norris. Tackling the Dailys was a job for a posse, or the Arizona Rangers, not for me — not solo.

Dennis Daily had his revolver out and had stuck it under Norris's chin. John and Grover Daily were laughing. Norris seemed to be pleading. I pulled my handbill from my pocket to make sure I'd read it correctly.

I didn't want to profit from a killing, but if Dennis Daily pulled that trigger, I doubt he'd stick around to bury Norris, and I knew he wouldn't take him in for the bounty. Just as I was thinking about the situation, Dennis pulled the gun away from Norris and I checked the handbill. Alive. Good.

Dennis and Norris shook hands. John and Grover commenced to head for the back of the stable where Norris had the bulk of his supplies.

About two minutes passed before Grover was back in sight. He had what appeared to be a sugar sack in his hand. He showed it to Dennis, then dumped the contents on the ground.

The coins shone in the sunlight. Maybe a few hundred dollars. But knowing the Daily's reputation, it was enough to warrant shedding blood. It seemed like by giving up his score, Norris had scored a few more days of breathing – and the few coins Dennis Daily had left on the ground.

Now, as I waited, I thought, *if the Dailys ride off with their bounty, so will I.*

I figured Norris would be so shook up over the matter that, once alone, he'd make a mistake. I was in the position for that mistake to be me.

Sure enough, with most of the gold coins back in the sac, Dennis Daily stowed it in his saddle bag. The Dailys mounted, tipped their hats and laughed as Norris picked up the few discarded coins, looked at his paltry profit, his shoulders giving way to defeat.

Dennis led his gang toward the west, topped the ridge, and never looked back.

I kept watch as Norris seemingly fell to a sitting position, took off his hat and hung his head. That was my cue.

It's not an easy task to draw a gun when you're sitting on the ground. I've practiced it, and while I'm fairly quick and accurate while standing, I'm slow and a bit wide when shooting from the ground. I'd have to practice more.

I left my horse and eased my way toward Norris. I was within about twenty yards when he finally looked up. But he didn't look in my direction, so I crept closer. He appeared to be staring at the stable. He whistled. His horse ambled around the side of the stable and stopped. The horse stomped three times as he eyed me. That got Norris' attention, but too late.

I ran the last few yards and had my gun on Norris before he could react. I grinned. Norris shook his head and laughed. "So, what is a little fish going to do with a whale?"

I pulled the handbill from my pocket, snapped it to get it unfolded, then tapped my loaded gun on the spot that had his price. Five-hundred wasn't much of a bounty, but it was a start. The most Norris had ever done was rob a few travelers. It might not have gotten much attention if the one traveler hadn't been a man of God taking money to the downtrodden in Tombstone.

Once I had Norris in Benson, I let the sheriff take over. I took my five-hundred dollars, got a good meal at Café Bonita, and did some asking around about that man of God.

I found that priest just outside Saint Paul's Episcopal Church in Tombstone. He was tending to some geraniums and petunias. I pulled the reward money out of my pocket, peeled off three-hundred and fifty dollars and handed it to him. I figured it would more than make up for the two hundred he'd lost.

He thanked me, then eyed the wad of cash I still had in my hand.

He stood back to take in my stature, laughed, then challenged me to a boxing match for the rest of the bounty.

I'm back to fishing.

A Murder of Crows

A Travis Cooper Tale

If anyone in the crowd had let their curiosity linger on someone besides the condemned, they might have noticed the smug look of satisfaction on the fat man's face. He was the only spectator who had smirked when the drifter defecated as he danced the dead man's waltz. I singled out the fat man at once.

A day might have made a difference, but a drifter has little hope for defense and less for alibis, and I had only suspicion instead of solid evidence that would have placed indecision in the minds of the accusers. But now, I had a face and someone to follow, and a vow of vindication for those in the wake of the fat man's violation. And in a town as small as Willcox, ascertaining the man's name, and those of any henchmen, would be a cinch. The motive might prove more difficult.

The batwings creaked and my attention turned from the onlookers as they posed with the deceased to the man up on the boardwalk behind me. "Mornin'. Always heard this town was friendly." I turned back toward the gallows and the overly eager photographer. "Hope that's not an indication that I've been led wrong."

The bartender wiped his hands on his apron, stepped down beside me and watched the crowd for a moment, then shook his head and sighed. "Around here, you usually get what you give, but that's all the law would allow. After what he did, he should have been quartered." He brushed his hands together as a sign that he wanted to be finished with the matter. "Well, now. I'm gonna get real busy, so if you're wantin' a drink, you might wanna get a head start." He looked me up and down and scowled. "You old enough for a drink?"

I pushed my hat off my brow. "Depends on who you ask."

He chuckled and offered his hand. “Grover Tillis.”

I shook his hand firmly. “Travis Cooper.”

Grover wiped out a glass, set it in front of me and poured the first shot.

“So, what was he guilty of?”

He turned his attention to polishing the top of the bar, slowly moving away from me. “Murdered a family. Ned and Sally Odom along with their two little ones. Kenny was workin’ on six and Joanie tagged along behind him wherever he went. Hired that drifter to help with the harvest. Had to get them apples to market in a hurry so he could pay his mortgage.” He shook his head and sighed. “Woulda been their last payment. They woulda owned them orchards free and clear.” He looked at his pocket watch. “Well, he’s been hangin’ thirty minutes. They’ll cut the son of a bitch down now. I better get some bottles filled.”

This little bit of information, along with what I’d learned in the last two towns after the last murders, gave me a way in. And the Arizona Ranger who walked up beside me would be my way out. He started to say something and I shifted my weight from one foot to the other and glared at him in the mirror, then hung my head as I twirled my shot glass.

Grover flung his rag over his shoulder and came back to fill the ranger’s request, then tapped his finger on the bar beside my glass. “Aren’t you gonna drink that?”

I downed the shot, wiped my mouth on my shirtsleeve, then wiped my eyes with my hands.

“You all right, Son?”

I stared into my empty glass. “I reckon not. Sally was my half-sister. Ned sent for me about a month ago. Just took a while to get here. Mama’s gonna take this real hard. She’s been so excited about movin’ here and helpin’ with the little ones. Guess I should sell out and go on back home.” I sniffled and inhaled.

“There’s nothin’ to sell, Son. They was killed before Ned made that last payment. Them apples never got to market.”

“You think the man at the bank would give me a little more time?”

"Wasn't a bank loan. It was a personal agreement. You'd have to take that up with Mr. Sexton."

I pulled a Morgan from my pocket and slid it across the bar. With one finger, Grover slid it back to me, then refilled my glass, patted my hand and made his way to the other end of the bar to serve the first of the spectators.

As men trudged through the batwings, the Arizona Ranger beside me kept his attention on the reflections in the mirror in front of him, occasionally stopping on mine. I'd met Robert just a couple of months back while I was searching for my father's killer, and although Robert was seven years my senior, we had quickly become friends. Robert took off his hat, ran his fingers through curly brown hair, then snugged his hat back in place. "So... whaddya think?"

"Know anything about apples?"

He smiled. "Well, now... known a couple bad ones. Had you pegged that way."

"What changed your mind?"

"Well, now... not sure I have. Just wanna be on your good side. I've seen your handiwork."

"If you draw that pistol as slow as you talk, you'd do best to stay behind me."

His chuckle was slow and deep. "Have to talk slow. Don't want you gettin' lost if I start usin' big words."

One of the patrons in the mirror's reflection caught my attention and I nudged Robert. "See the fat man in the suit?"

Robert's grin faded. "Sure. Think he knows anything about apples?"

"Maybe."

"You first?"

"Give me about ten minutes."

I knocked timidly on the open door and peeked in. "'Scuse me... Sheriff?"

From the chair behind a desk piled high with papers and books, a man of about thirty peered over the top of his glasses. "I never could stand to see a man swing." He held up a book. "Thought maybe a few chapters of Mark Twain might get it out of my mind." He marked his page with a feather and gently placed the book on one of the piles and stood. "What can I do for you?"

I sighed and hung my head. "Guess I'm not sure."

He walked to the front of his desk. "Why don't we start with names. I'm Sheriff here in Willcox. Sheriff Cray. And who might you be?"

I accepted his proffered hand. "Travis Cooper, Sir—Sally's half-brother. Maybe if I'd got here sooner this wouldn't have happened."

"I'm sorry, Travis. I didn't realize the Odoms' had any family." He tipped his head and one eye narrowed just a bit. "How did you hear about this?"

"I didn't, Sir. Ned sent for me a while back, but he didn't mention gettin' here in time for pickin' apples. Just said they was settled in real good and wanted Mama and me join 'em. But I reckon if I'd been here, they wouldn't have hired that fella and..." I looked at the floor and let out a sorrowful sigh. "...they wouldn't be... and the little ones wouldn't...."

"Is your mother here?"

I looked him in the eye. "No, Sir. She sent me on ahead so Ned and me could get a room added on before winter." I hung my head again. "Mr. Tillis over at the saloon told me when I asked about...." I hooked my thumb toward the gallows, then looked him in the eye again. "I think I need to head on up there and see if I can figure a way to get them apples to market. Maybe the man holdin' the deed will see clear to give me a couple days to make this right."

"That would be Sid Sexton, but you'd better have a talk with him soon. He's a shrewd business man and I'm sure he's already looking for a buyer. He can't make money if that land is sitting idle." He turned his attention toward the door and the man occupying the space between there and the boardwalk. "Is there something I can help you with?"

"Well... Sheriff... there is." Robert took off his hat and extended his hand. "Captain Robert Fitzsimmons, sir, Arizona Ranger. I'd like a private word with you."

Cray sized him up, then turned to me. "Travis, you go on over to the hotel and ask for Mr. Sexton. If he gives the go-ahead, I'll find someone to escort you up to the Odom place."

At the hotel, I didn't want to appear complacent, so I sat on the edge of the chair and rubbed my hands together as I waited for the hotel clerk to summon Mr. Sexton. I hadn't told the clerk who I was, nor whom I professed to be. I wanted to see the look on Sexton's face when that little bit of news came out. I couldn't have been more pleased when the fat man sauntered down the steps and was ushered in my direction. *This shouldn't take long. Not long at all.*

He smiled and extended his hand. "Sidney Sexton. What can I do for you, young man?"

I looked at his hand for a moment before accepting it. "Travis Cooper, Sir. I'm...." I hung my head. "I was... Sally's half-brother." I shook my head. "I just can't believe...."

Sexton put his hand on my shoulder and I looked him in the eye. His face softened and his voice was sorrowful. "I'm so sorry. I didn't know she had any family besides Ned and the little ones. Will you join me for dinner and you can tell me why you wished to speak with me?"

This wasn't what I expected, but I went ahead with my plan and I figured I'd better mention the law so he wouldn't suspect anything but the truth from me. "Sheriff Cray said you was the one holdin' the mortgage. I was wantin' to know if you'd extend the time just a little. Maybe I could get them apples to market and make that last payment."

"I have to be honest. I have a prospective buyer." He rubbed his chin. "But he wanted a couple more beers and I make it a habit not to conduct business in a saloon, so please take me up on my offer and we'll discuss this over dinner. I'll meet you back here in an hour."

As I walked onto the boardwalk, I had to wonder. Was Sexton going to set me up for that final payment, then find a way to do away with me and still keep his new buyer? Or, was he innocent? I needed more information from the last two towns, but for now, besides the saloon, I had a good view of the telegraph office, the jailhouse, and a few businesses, so I took a seat. Maybe I'd find out where Sexton did business before we met again for dinner.

I took a small tin from my pocket, opened it, retrieved a piece of hard candy and popped it into my mouth and wondered if Robert would come back with any useful information. I didn't have to wait long. I pushed my hat off my brow and looked up at him. "You look a little rattled."

"Yeah... I suppose I am." He shook his head and took a seat in the chair beside me. He took a moment to get settled. "Trav... I told him I'd share what I found out... not only about the murders... but about you, too."

"So, you didn't tell him about me?"

"No... I think everybody needs to think you're who you say you are, for the time being, but when we get this figured out, I'll keep my promise."

"You think he's an honest lawman?"

"Well... seems genuine to me."

"That's all I need." I crossed my arms and sighed. "So, what do you know so far?"

"Sheriff Cray is pretty sure they hung the right man, but I see too many holes in that theory. We're going out there whether the money man gives you permission, or not. Cray gave me the go ahead and I told him I'd be responsible for you. Well, now... who's the money man?"

I smiled. "The fat man."

"So... what did he say?"

"He's meetin' me back here for dinner. I think you should join us. Introduce yourself proper and see if he flinches."

"Whaddya read so far?"

I shook my head. "Can't say for sure. Seems to be sympathetic about the whole thing. But if anybody knows about puttin' on a show...."

Robert's chuckle lasted a full five seconds. "Yeah... but you never fooled me. Not one bit. Now... what's on your mind?"

"We need to know if the other murders tie in with land deals and private mortgages, and if so, who holds that title then and now. It's a hell of a scheme if the fat man is killin' off the payees before they can make that final payout. He gets the land back, resells it for today's market value and lives high on the hog. Might just explain why Sexton had such a smug look on his face at the hangin'. He got his land back and somebody else paid for his crimes."

"Now... here's what I'm thinking. We gotta find out a little about that drifter... see if he was around when the other murders happened." Robert sighed. "I'll get a few inquiries heading in the right direction and talk to the banker."

"Why the banker?"

He grinned and I knew it was because I'd had to ask. "Well... they don't like competition. If there's more private loans out there, the banker will know who's holding and who's paying. Might wanna talk to a few of those who are paying and find out what they think of their lender."

Robert stood and I looked up at him. I was working toward seventeen and still growing, but I knew I'd never be eye to eye with him. I was close to five-ten and couldn't tip a scale past a hundred and fifty after a six-course meal and a gallon of beer. At six-three and a couple hundred pounds, Robert made an impression on most that saw him, and while I was always trail-worn and dirty, Robert was always clean shaven, never had a hair out of place and never had a crease where it wasn't intended. He tipped his hat. "I'll be back to interrupt your dinner."

In the course of my conversation with Robert, Sexton had gone in and out of the telegraph office and the sheriff's office. Now I had to figure out if he was making inquiries about me, or trying to cover up any loose ends.

The waiter handed me a menu and Sexton nodded. "Order anything you like. It's on me."

"Chops and potatoes." I handed the menu back to the waiter and worked on getting Sexton where I wanted him. "Was the Arizona Ranger your idea or the sheriff's?"

"What Ranger?"

"The one that said he's gonna escort me to the farm once he gets the go-ahead from you. Said he had some work to do, then he'd be joinin' us."

Sexton looked up at the waiter. "Same thing and coffee." He waited for the waiter to leave. "Wasn't my idea, but it's a good idea. I sure don't want to go back out there and it would be best for someone to be with you."

"Have you been thinkin' on my request?"

"That I have. You go on out there and have a look around, then come back and tell me if you think you can handle the job. If you think you can get those apples to market and make that payment in say... two weeks' time, then it's yours. If not, I'll have to honor the other buyer. That fruit won't last long once it hits the ground." His gaze shifted to the entrance. "That must be your ranger." He waved him over.

"Robert Fitzsimmons, sir. Captain, Arizona Rangers. Pleased to make your acquaintance."

Sexton pointed to an empty chair. "Sit and join us." He raised his arm to hail the waiter, then waited until Robert gave his order. "I appreciate you taking this young man out to the farm. If you've spoken to Sheriff Cray, you'll understand why I'm grateful."

"Well... yes... I have and I do. I'll explain it to Travis on the way out there. I'd leave right after we eat, but I'm waiting for word about two other murders in this part of the territory."

"Then you'll be investigating me as well. I've lost two other accounts in the last couple of months, so don't think I haven't tried to figure this out on my own, because I have. If those accounts had been paid and clear, I'd retire and stop this business of selling land. The missus would rather I was home."

"Why not sell it to the bank and let them do the work?"

"Most young couples can't afford those interest rates and deadlines. I don't sell for any cheaper than market value, but I make allowances for bad years and unexpected expenses. No. I'd rather go on working than to see the bank, or some New York swindler, take advantage of these good people."

"I'll tell you what I find out unless I found out something you're not telling me."

Sexton nodded. "Fair enough."

Robert kept a pencil and paper next to his plate and wrote down anything he thought might help the investigation. I feigned indifference to anything that didn't have to do with my supposed half-sister. I was eating dessert when they finally took some interest in the food in front of them. Once they were through, Robert looked at me.

"Now... Travis.... You need to let Mr. Sexton and me have a private word. You take your coffee on out to the front room and I'll meet you there in a bit."

I stiffened up. "But—"

"I won't be long."

I pouted. "Yes, Sir."

I stomped out. I wanted to make sure Sexton sized me up as an immature, hard-headed kid that could be easily bamboozled, so I crossed my arms and furrowed my brow as I sat and watched them from a very comfortable, overstuffed, but well-worn chair that faced the dining area. I thought about how to introduce my gun. I'd always carried an old pistol in my saddle bag and wore it if need be. I'd leave that gun hidden and I'd wear a brand-new one on my brand-new gun belt.

After about fifteen minutes, Robert and Sexton stood and shook hands. I stood so Sexton would know that I had indeed kept my attention on their little meeting. Robert did his *I'm in charge* saunter with Sexton not far behind.

"Now... Travis, I'm gonna get a room and you can sleep on the floor. You got a bedroll?"

I stood up straight and smiled. "Yes, Sir! I'll go get it right away!" *Showtime.*

They were still talking when I came back in with my bedroll over my shoulder and my brand-new gun and holster buckled high on my waist. "I'm ready!"

Robert chuckled a bit. "Well... I know what you plan on doing with that bedroll, but what the heck you gonna do with that gun?"

I reached for it and Robert had his pistol under my chin before my hand touched steel. Wide-eyed, I put my hands in the air and stood on my toes. "I was just gonna show you it was empty!"

Robert narrowed his eyes and pushed the pistol harder into my chin. "An empty gun will get you just as dead as a loaded one! Now, you're gonna listen to me and listen good! For the next couple days, you're my responsibility. Once we're out of town, I'll give you a lesson or two on how to go about not getting yourself killed. After this is over, you can get yourself killed and it won't be on me, but until then, we're doing it my way. Is that understood?"

I got another inch of height out of my toes. "Yes, Sir!"

He grabbed my pistol from the holster, then put his back. "And for Christ's sake, loosen that damn gun belt! You look like a skinny whore wearing a leather corset!"

I unbuckled my gun belt and let it fall just below my waist, looked at Robert for approval, then fastened it in place. "Can I have my pistol back?"

"Have you ever shot it before?"

"Haven't had the need."

"And you won't as long as you're with me. You'll get it tomorrow."

I looked down. "Yes, Sir."

Sexton patted me on the shoulder. "I believe you're in good hands. You come see me when you get back from the farm."

I smiled. "Yes, Sir."

I stayed by Robert's side while he checked in. I put my bedroll in the room, but I proudly wore my empty holster, like an idiot I was portraying, the rest of the afternoon as I followed along behind Robert. He dropped off his clothes to be laundered, then headed to the barber shop. I was sure he wanted to be impeccable at our evening meal and I was curious as to how he managed such luxury on a ranger's pay. So, when we sat to eat, I asked just that question.

He explained. "My mother was one of the first women to pitch a tent at the start of the gold rush."

With my mouth open, I held my heaped-up fork midair.

He chuckled. "No... she cooked, they ate. She made a small fortune, married a haberdasher and had me. A man has to eat and he has to dress. I know how to do both. A man has to die, too, so I suppose I could have gone into undertaking."

I ate the food on my fork and went for more. "So, you packed up all your gold and came to the territory to serve justice?"

"When you don't have to work for a living you can work at what you like. I thought about sheriffing, but I don't like staying in one place too long. Rangering lets me enforce the law without staying in one place too long."

I grinned. "Guess that keeps you outta trouble with the women."

He grinned. "What do you know about women?"

I gazed toward the door. "I know a fine lookin' one when I see one and that's about the finest I've seen in a while."

He followed my gaze and shook his head. "Hard to keep up with a woman like that, and even if you could... well... she's probably got a husband, or a rich daddy who won't be far behind."

I chewed on a piece of steak and watched her for a moment. She caught me, and with my cheeks full of meat, I smiled. She feigned a smile, then stared at Robert. His indifference didn't please her. She huffed, then picked up her skirts and approached the waiter. I went back to my steak and potatoes.

Robert sat back in his chair. "Well... look there, what'd I tell you?"

"Damn. His wife or his daughter?"

"Well... might just be the reason Sexton's wife would rather he stayed home. If the wife has expensive tastes like the girlfriend, and he's trying to keep them both happy, or at least this one so she doesn't cause problems, then he's gotta keep the bankroll high."

"Or—" I put up one finger to stop Robert from interrupting. "Now, hear me out. The wife *does* know about the girlfriend, so she's framing him for the murders." I filled my fork and shrugged. "A woman scorned."

Robert chuckled. "You'd do best to keep that in mind when you get a little older." Robert stood and I stared up at her like a love-struck teenager and waited for him to correct me. "Travis."

"Oh!" I stood up. "'Scuse me, Ma'am. Guess I was daydreamin'."

She looked down at my empty holster, then turned to Robert. “It’s Miss. Miss Sexton.”

Mr. Sexton put his hand on the small of her back. “This is my daughter, Lizbeth. Lizbeth, this is Robert and Travis. They’ll be going to the farm tomorrow.”

She smiled sweetly at both of us. “Are you going to purchase that homestead? I’m sure Daddy will offer it at a fair price. Of course, he’ll expect a ten percent down-payment.”

“Now, Lizbeth, you leave the particulars to me. Do the two of you mind if we join you?”

Robert pulled out a chair for Lizbeth and we all sat. Robert waited patiently for their food to arrive, but I immediately dug back into mine and was on dessert before they had a plate in front of them. That's one of the benefits of playing the dumb kid.

Lizbeth pushed back from the table. “If you’ll excuse me, please. I’ll be right back.”

Robert and Mr. Sexton stood and I knocked my chair over trying to accommodate, fumbled to right it, then sat back down with an exhausted look on my face. “Ma’am... I mean, Miss, I hope you don’t mind, but I’m gonna stay put when you come back.”

“Suit yourself.”

Robert watched her leave, then sat back down. “Now... Mr. Sexton, does she know who I am?”

“She’s only just arrived. I haven’t gotten that far.”

“Then I suggest you leave it at that. No offense, but women tend to talk and the less interference and the more untainted information I get, the better it will be for you, as long as you’re not guilty of anything—land fraud or otherwise.”

“I’d rather she didn’t know that you were investigating, and that the investigation included me, so you’ll get no argument here. I hesitate to tell her about Travis having a claim on that farm, as well. I think that bit of information should be kept quiet until this is resolved.” He smiled. “And there’s my lovely daughter, again. We’ll find another subject to discuss over dessert.”

Our company retired for the evening and Robert decided that a beer wasn't inappropriate, but he made me leave my empty holster in the room. He chuckled. "There's no limit to your eagerness to appear ignorant, is there?"

"I'd drag my knuckles and scratch myself in public if it meant we'd catch a killer. And besides, havin' me around makes you look good."

"Well... just one beer, keep your ears open, and do what you do best."

At four a.m., we were the only ones in the dining room. The waiter yawned as he took our order, but I was pleased to discover that the cook must have been wide awake because the aroma of fresh coffee, bacon frying, and what I was sure would be hot, flaky biscuits, wafted out of the kitchen.

Food ordered and a quiet room gave us time to discuss the day. I started the conversation. "The daughter is a little smug. And she seems like she might understand the business. Think she could have had a hand in this?"

"I was wondering about her. Maybe when we get back from the farm, we'll ask about having a meal with Sexton and her. See how curious she is about what we might have found out there."

Four fresh, unmarked graves occupied the ground near the garden that appeared to have been well kept. The last of the tomatoes and berries, now a feast for the birds.

Inside the small, clapboard house the smell of death still hung in the air. Dried blood was smeared across the kitchen floor and toward two smaller rooms. Inside the larger of the two, I checked for any clues that might have been missed or ignored. Robert checked the kitchen.

"Hey, Robert. Finding anything?"

"Not yet. Well, maybe. Got a box here with new dishes. Might be something."

I went to the kitchen and picked up one of the bowls from the package Robert had found and wasn't sure if it had anything to do with anything. I went back to my search in the children's room. Under one of the two small beds was a box. I pulled it out and checked the contents. "Hey, Robert! I think I got something!"

Robert came in from the other room and I showed him the contents of the box. He looked at the book and coloring sticks and said, "I guess I need an explanation."

"These might seem like an innocent thing to find in a child's room... if the children come from a family who can afford them. There must be, well, let me count... twelve of these books and two tins full of..." I looked at the label. "...Crayola crayons. I don't think the Odoms would have bought all of this if they needed money for the mortgage."

"So, you think this has something to do with the murder?"

"Not sure. Gotta think on it and see what we find out when we get back to town. Did you send telegrams to the other towns where the murders happened?"

"Sure did, but no answers yet."

"Might wanna send another to ask about books, crayons and dishes. Have them search the children's rooms. And the murder scenes that didn't involve children, look for anything else that might be extravagant for a farmer with a mortgage due. Let's see if there's anything in the outbuildings that might be a clue. And I guess we better have an answer about those apples."

Back in town, Robert and I went to the sheriff's office to see if what we found might have a bearing on the murders. When I walked in, I noticed the pile of books on his desk. "You read all them?"

He chuckled and set aside the book he'd been reading. "Not yet. I do have a town to watch over." He turned to Robert for the information since I wasn't supposed to have the brains for such things. "Find anything of interest out there, Captain?"

"Books and dishes."

"Books?"

"For children. Pictures to color."

"What do books have to do with murder? Or dishes?"

"Not sure they have anything to do with murder. But not sure how the Odoms could afford to spend the money on them either."

"Maybe check with Fred over at the mercantile. He'll know if they've been buying children's books or dishware."

Robert nodded. "Will do. Thank you, Sheriff." Back on the boardwalk, Robert leaned toward me and we both said it at the same time. "Or who else might have bought them."

I chuckled. "Books. Maybe it's a schoolmarm."

Robert stopped dead in his tracks and turned to look at me. "That's interesting. But, still... the cost of the books." He started walking again. I quick-paced to keep up with him.

At the mercantile, Robert spoke to the owner. "The sheriff said you might have some insight about coloring books... and crayons. Do you sell them here? And if so, did the Odoms ever purchase any?"

"I don't recollect anyone purchasing any. I've had several here for a couple weeks, but I haven't displayed them yet. I suppose I should."

"Where did you get your order from?

"Let me have a look at my book." Fred pulled a ledger from beneath the counter. "Ah, yes. Crayola wax crayons came from Easton, Pennsylvania. Back there they sell for about a nickel, but I have to cover shipping. So, I'll sell for about seven cents for a box of eight colors. The books to color came out of New York City." He looked up at Robert. "Does that help any?"

"I think it does. Thank you, Fred."

Back to the boardwalk and another back and forth between Robert and me. I said, "Well, I think maybe the telegraph office to see if there's any news, and the post office to see if anybody here got packages from Pennsylvania or New York."

Robert nodded and chuckled. "You sure you don't wanna be a ranger?"

I laughed. "Too many rules, and I'd have to justify what I already know if there's to be an honest outcome, so to speak. Nope, I'll just keep using you for the brawn, badge and good looks, and I'll be the idiot kid with all the answers."

Robert sent out telegrams to the two towns with similar murders and had one answer within an hour. "Books, crayons, and new dishware just like the Odom's. We'll sit on this and wait on the other sheriffs to reply. Let's go to the dining room and get something to eat. Maybe Sexton and his daughter will be there. See if the daughter has any questions she doesn't need answers for."

I fell back into my idiot routine when we entered the dining room. Sexton was there with his daughter and waved us over.

Seated, we took care of the pleasantries, then ordered. Lizbeth was the first to speak about the Odom murder. "It's just awful, isn't it? Why those two little ones must have been scared to death when that drifter started shooting!"

I hung my head and sniffled.

Sexton patted his daughter on the arm and said, "Now, Lizbeth, they were Travis' family. I think we can find something else to talk about over this fine meal."

She huffed a bit. "Whatever you say, Daddy."

Talk turned to sunny, cloudy, rain or no rain, throughout the rest of the meal. My thoughts turned from the weather to whether or not the drifter even had a gun. Robert noted the contemplation on my face and excused us as soon as our meal was done.

We headed for the saloon and Robert said, "So, what's on your mind, Travis?"

"Did anyone ever question whether the drifter did indeed own a gun? Or... have access to one? Did he have a gun when he was arrested?"

Robert stopped and turned toward the sheriff's office.

Cray was filing paperwork when we walked in. "What can I do for you, Robert?"

"Can I see that report on the arrest of the drifter?"

"Sure thing. Just getting ready to file it. What are you thinking?"

"I thought there was a hole or two in the report, but just couldn't fill them in at the time." Robert took the report and read it to himself, then looked up at the Sheriff. "Where is the gun the drifter used? He should have had it on him. And what motive would he have had? I doubt the Odoms had much of value, so robbery doesn't fit. He gained nothing but rope from this, and did it all without a gun to show for it. Says here, he reported the murders. Why would he do that if he committed them? He might have been guilty of a hanging offense somewhere along the line, but not here, and not murder. Seems awful convenient that in each of the other two towns, there was always a drifter to take the fall."

"You think maybe someone is finding jobs for these men then setting them up?"

"I can't think of any other way to reason it out."

I had been listening to Robert and Cray, but also observing what I could through the open door. Lizbeth had passed by, soon after we had arrived. I moved to the doorway and stepped onto the boardwalk and feigned a yawn while putting my hands on my hips and stretching backward. I brought my arms to my side and shook them as if trying to wake up. I adjusted my empty holster on my gun belt and turned to go back inside. I had acted like I hadn't seen her sitting on a nearby bench when I came out, but stopped to acknowledge her on the way in. "Howdy, Miss Sexton. Fine day, ain't it?"

She huffed and put her nose in the air. "I think I heard enough about the weather at dinner. I've been shopping and decided I needed a rest. I think I'm ready to continue on with my day." With that, she stood and meandered toward the shops.

I took a seat on the bench she had just vacated and pretended to nod off, but kept one eye partially alert. She turned once to look my way, most likely to rule out me observing her, then she turned and headed to the telegraph office.

Robert exited the sheriff's office and took up a seat beside me. "So, what are you up to?"

"Lizbeth was sitting here while you and Cray were having your discussion. I thought I might be able to rattle her. She said she was resting from shopping and decided to continue on, but she went to the telegraph office. See, no... don't look... she just came out. And notice, she doesn't have any packages from her morning of shopping."

"She probably paid to have them delivered. We'll wait a couple minutes until she's outta sight, then go talk to the telegrapher. Might have a few messages waiting for me, anyhow."

We waited for a bit, saw her go into the hotel, then we hit the boardwalk for the telegraph office. Robert had two waiting for him. He explained the contents to me. "One acknowledged books and crayons. The other murder victims had no children, but there was a package that had been opened, but the contents intact. It was dishware. The message goes on to say that the couple already had plenty of dishes, but old and chipped."

Robert waved me outside, then said, "So, looks like someone is getting close to these families before they're murdered. But how does a drifter always happen to be there to take the blame?"

"And what of the telegram that Lizbeth sent?"

"Damn, got interested in mine and didn't ask."

He went back inside and had the telegrapher show him the message Lizbeth had sent.

He joined me on the boardwalk, then smiled and said, "Seems she thinks I'm quite handsome. Just letting her *sister* know her daddy is doing well and they've been taking meals with a very handsome man. I doubt she means you." He nodded toward the door. "Let's walk."

"Looks and brawn. Told you. She didn't mention your occupation, did she?"

"No. Not a word." Robert spoke quietly. "I think we need to have supper with the Sextons. Find out more about this other daughter. Margaret Sexton. I sent a telegram to get some background on her. We should know shortly."

The telegrapher ran up behind us. Robert turned and accepted the message. He explained the contents to me. "Margaret Sexton managed a bank until she was accused of stealing from some of the bigger accounts. She left and her father paid it back so they wouldn't prosecute. Maybe we should find out who manages the money for Sexton. Seems there's a bad apple and it's not just the ones rotting on the ground at the Odom orchard."

Robert left a message of an invitation at the desk, and we headed upstairs to freshen up for supper. Well, Robert freshened with a clean shirt and a face wash, and a bit of organization of toiletries. I spent the time organizing my thoughts.

We headed back down for supper and to see if Sexton had received Robert's invitation. Sure enough, Sexton was at a table waiting for our arrival. Lizbeth, nowhere in sight.

I adjusted my empty holster on my gun belt and plopped down in a chair. Robert nodded a hello to Sexton and joined me at the table. Robert said, "Will your daughter be joining us?"

"She'll be along. Seems she had an errand to do at the last minute." He chuckled. "I don't know about that girl. Seems to want to know every detail about my business. One daughter in the business is enough. I don't need her meddling, as well."

I remained seemingly uninterested in the mention of a second daughter. Robert started the questioning. "So, you have two daughters?"

"Two is more than any man needs." He chuckled. "Or can afford."

"Is she with you on this trip?"

"No. She lives in Phoenix. She takes care of my interests, and runs a halfway house. She finds work for those in need." He chuckled then sighed. "She's atoning for past sins. Had to pull her out of a mess in Denver. Nothing I'd care to talk about. It's been handled. Now, let's talk about more pleasant things. Ah, and there's my Lizbeth!" He smiled as both he and Robert stood to welcome Lizbeth to the table. I stayed seated as per my idiot character.

Lizbeth seemed a bit flustered and just as she sat, Robert was summoned to the desk. The clerk nodded toward the door and I leaned my head in their direction and was able to discern the conversation that passed between them. "The telegrapher just left this for you. Said to make sure you got it right away. Said the other party has already received a copy."

"Thank you. Can you send someone over with menus? I think we're ready to order."

When Robert returned, I glanced at him and he shook his head in a *not now* kinda way. We ordered and had light conversation throughout, but Lizbeth was preoccupied with something other than supper. Her face showed concern, and her appetite was lean.

Robert shattered her concentration when he said, "Well, I think they hung the right man. I have another assignment I need to look into."

I sat back, put my fork on my plate and sighed. "I just don't see how I'm gonna be able to make that harvest. I don't have the know-how, or the labor to do it. I think I'll have to head back and let Mama know we're stayin' put. I have a job back there, and we have a place to live. We'll be all right without my sister's farm, and bein' up here would upset Mama." I stood, adjusted my empty holster on my gun belt, nodded and headed upstairs. Robert stayed behind to say a proper goodbye... for now.

Once in the room, Robert explained the telegram Lizbeth had received from Margaret. "Margaret wants Lizbeth to keep an eye on the sale of the Odom place. Says there might be another property to look into. I think Lizbeth is starting to piece all this together and doesn't want any part of it. Lizbeth might be self-centered, but I don't think she's a killer."

We loaded our horses at the Willcox station and boarded in separate cars so no one who might be watching would think we were traveling together. We'd join up again in Phoenix, much like we had in Willcox.

I walked into the sheriff's office. "Are you the sheriff here in Phoenix?" He held back a laugh when he noticed my empty holster in my brand-new gun belt that I had cinched high on my waist.

"Yes, Sheriff Grady. Can I help you, son?"

"I just come up from Willcox. Heard down there that there's a place I could get a free meal and maybe a line on a job. Been lookin' for a while now. Mama needs the money for rent. I can't let her down."

He looked around me. "Where is your mama?"

"She's down around Benson. No work down there right now. Everybody's been hired that's needed for the season. I do know a bit about cows, so ranch work would be okay."

"There's a halfway house about five blocks from here. North two blocks and over three. Ask for Margaret. She always has a line on ranch and farm work all over the territory. She'll get you set up with a meal and bed if she doesn't have work for you right away."

"Thanks, Sheriff. I'll do that. I gotta make Mama proud." I hung my head and walked out just as Robert walked into the telegraph office across the street. We'd planned on meeting at the saloon closest to the train station. That was back two blocks, so I headed toward the halfway house, circled around the block and back toward the saloon.

The few patrons in the saloon laughed when I walked in. I guess my idiot disguise was still working. The bartender looked me up and down, then asked, "You old enough to drink, boy?"

"Don't know if I'm old enough, but I'm miserable enough. And worried."

"What's a young fella, like you, got to be worried about?"

"Findin' a job to help my mama. Papa run off and took my younger brother with him. Doted on him all the time. Papa never liked me much. Always said I was worthless. But mama needs my help. She needs money for food and rent. Papa left us with nothin' but bills."

The bartender set a glass on the counter. "My name's Martin. What'll you have? It's on me."

I feigned surprise. "Oh, I can't accept that. I got enough for a glass of water." I dug my hand into my pocket.

"Water's free." He poured a mug of beer and set it in front of me. "The beer is on me. Don't think you could handle whiskey."

"Thank you, Mr. Martin." I took a sip and coughed, got my eyes to water a bit and wiped my mouth with my sleeve. Martin laughed, then went on to the next customer. It was Robert. He stood at the bar, just a few feet from me.

Robert nodded in my direction and chuckled as he spoke to Martin loud enough for me to hear the conversation. "He's a little young. Looks like a skinny whore in a leather corset with that gun belt of his."

Martin laughed. "Sure does, but seems like a good kid. He's here to get a job to help his mama."

Robert looked at me in the mirror. "Hey, kid. You need a meal? I'm about to eat after I finish this beer."

"Oh, I can't ask you to do that, Mister. I'll manage."

"I insist. I wanna hear your story and find out why you have a gun belt and no gun. There's gotta be a story there." He laughed.

"I suppose, if you just want some company, I'll accept. But if I get a job, I'll be takin' you to supper once I get Mama settled with rent and food money."

"Down that beer and let's go."

I downed my beer, and wide-eyed, I shivered and shook my head. "Maybe I'd better stick to water from here on out."

Robert had already gotten a room, so when we entered the dining hall, we were immediately seated. He accepted both menus, handed one to me and looked around the room. "Well, what do you have going?"

"I can get a bed and job possibilities at the halfway house. I'm supposed to see Margaret. Guess once she has a position she thinks would suit me, you'll find out if there's a mortgage and who the lender might be and if books and dishes works into the mix. Right?"

"Sounds like we're on the same page. You still sure you don't wanna be a ranger?"

I chuckled. "I keep telling you—too many rules."

"Well, the offer is out there, and I'd vouch for you."

"Well, look who's here! I'll bet that's Margaret in the doorway. Looks just like Lizbeth only a bit older. Guess it's time for the idiot to come out in me."

"I didn't know he left."

"Smartass. Shhhh. Here she comes."

"Excuse me, please." She looked at Robert and when he stood to greet her, she must have decided he didn't fit the profile. She looked at me, still seated, and said, "Are you the young man looking for work? I just spoke to the sheriff out on the boardwalk. He said a new boy in town was looking for work."

I rubbed my hands together then wiped them on my pants. "I suppose that would be me. Travis Cooper, ma'am. Need work to help my mama with food and rent back home in Benson." With the look of hope on my face, I asked, "Are you the halfway house lady."

She started to offer her hand, then must have thought better of it. "Yes, I'm Margaret Sexton. I run the place and I might have just the job for you." She turned to Robert. "Is he with you, sir?"

Robert chuckled. "No, Ma'am. Just met him at the saloon and he looked like he could use a good meal. Haven't gotten past names yet and I'm just passing through on my way to Flagstaff."

She smiled and looked a little relieved that I was indeed alone. "Well, Travis, if you want to come by the halfway house later this evening, I'll have a bed for you and a bowl of oatmeal if you're hungry. We can discuss work in the morning. I think I have just the thing for you." She hesitated and a look of concern flashed across her face. "Will your mama be joining you?"

"No. She won't travel, and I don't think she even knows how to get in touch with me. I'll send word and money when I have it."

Robert said, "I'll let him sleep on the floor in my room. I'll make sure he's up bright and early to meet you in the morning."

Margaret smiled. "I'm sure I have something for him. Thank you for your kindness, Robert. Travis, I'll see you later."

Robert sat and picked up his menu. "Well, since the telegram from Lizbeth to her and back were just pleasantries, I don't think Lizbeth is in on it, but as nervous as she seemed, maybe she's started to figure it out."

"So... I'll take that job and once we know where it is, we'll see who owns the ranch, if there's a mortgage and who holds it, how many payments are left and if there's somewhere nearby for you to hide out and cover my ass." I sat back in my chair and pondered. "I'm just wonderin' if Margaret does the shooting, or if she hires someone for that line of work. And are the gifts to distract? Or to get a foot in the door?"

"I guess we'll piece it together as it happens." Robert chuckled. "I bet you'll be out on the range when it happens. I'll have to do the dirty work."

"Oh, I'll head for the range, but I'll hide out close by. Has to be a building of some kind I can hole up in and keep an eye on things. I'll hide my business pistol in there and be ready for company. I doubt it will take more than a day or two to for the shooter to show up."

Margaret indeed had a job for me. She ushered me into the halfway house and fed me a huge bowl of oatmeal with milk. I glanced around the room and noted the coloring books and tin cans full of crayons on the long table beside me.

I finished my oatmeal, thanked Margaret, then listened as she gave me directions to my new job then sent me on my way. I had just left the town limits and had a nagging feeling I was being watched. A little further up the road and that feeling was still hanging with me. I turned in my saddle a few times, glanced around at my surroundings and didn't see anyone, but that didn't satisfy that nagging feeling.

As I rode through the Jackson's front gate, crows took to flight. They settled for a moment, then took to flight, again. Maybe whoever was following me had disrupted their momentary calm. I'd have to remain alert.

I soon learned that the Jacksons, whom I was now working for, had heard about growing cotton and had decided to try their luck at this new crop. Good thing. The crows, who announced my arrival, seemed to have found a home in the cornfield and were probably eating up most of the profit. I asked enough questions to find out that the Jacksons had two payments left on their mortgage, and Sexton was indeed the one who held their mortgage.

The problem the Jacksons faced was the usual. They needed help with the harvest so they could make those final payments and own this land free and clear.

One day at picking cotton and my back was sore and my fingers were bloody. But I kept a smile on my face knowing we'd soon have our mystery of murders unraveled. I just wasn't sure who would show up, and the circumstances had changed a bit. I couldn't hide out if I was picking cotton alongside the Jacksons and their young son, Junior, and I'd had no contact with Robert. Hopefully, the Jacksons would have me bed down in the barn, and hopefully, that's where I'd find Robert.

Late that afternoon, the crows took to flight, did a once over and settled again to eat up any profits the Jacksons might have gotten from the corn crop. I hoped they were announcing Robert's arrival and not the person who had dogged me.

A day of hard labor, or at least it was for me, and a meager meal of biscuits and salt ham, and I was exhausted. I wasn't used to this kind of work, or so little to eat afterward. I couldn't wait to wash off in the tank and bed down in the barn. And hopefully, Robert would be there. Indeed, he was.

Robert chuckled when he came out from behind a pile of corn husks. "You look a bit haggard."

I grabbed a husk. "What do you think they do with these?"

"I'd venture to say they make mattresses out of them."

"Well, I guess they get something out of that cornfield besides the sound of those crows. I guess I'll bed down with the husks. How 'bout you?"

"Already have my bedroll laid out."

"See anything suspicious while I was workin' my ass off?"

Robert laughed, "Yeah. You working your ass off. And those crows announcing my arrival. But not before I found out that the halfway house does order a lot of books and crayons. No idea about where the dishware comes from."

"Yep. I can vouch for the books and crayons and the bowl I ate out of looked the same as the dishware from the Odoms. I guess we can get some shut-eye. Since it seems there are always gifts involved, I think we can safely say that all is well, for now. Unless you've already gotten plenty of rest by sitting on your ass while you watch me work."

"I brought a few biscuits and some canned sausage and a jar of pickled eggs."

I yawned. "Supper was lean, but I'm too tired to chew. I'll have some in the morning."

Mr. Jackson rang the bell just before sunrise. I jumped up from my lumpy cornhusk bedding and met him at the water tank.

"How'd you sleep, Travis?"

"I put my bedroll on that pile of husks. Turns out, it's better than rocks." I laughed and wiped my face on the provided rag.

"I suppose a couple more hard days and we'll meet the next payment on this place. You up for it?"

"I'm ready when you are."

"Let's get a bite to eat before we get started."

Another meal of biscuits and salt ham and I was wishing I'd eaten some of the canned sausage and pickled eggs that Robert had offered me the previous evening.

Mrs. Jackson and Junior had gone in to fix a bit of dinner. It was coming on to noon and I was coming on to a bad back, bloody fingers and ears tired of those crow caws, when I saw a horse in the distance. I looked toward the loft in the barn and was glad to see Robert peering out from between a couple of broken boards. I turned to Mr. Jackson, then pointed to the rider. "You know who that is?"

Mr. Jackson looked to the sky, now black with crows, then put his hand above his eyes to shield them from the blazing sun. "Don't reckon I do. You keep on with it and I'll go let the Mrs. and Junior know we have company."

"I'll keep at it. Just ring that bell if you need me." I was worried about the Jacksons. I couldn't see the house from the cotton field and I wasn't sure if the rider would see me if I tried to sneak in for a better view. I thought it might be the murderer. I'd soon find out if Robert's and my plan worked out like we'd planned.

I waited until the rider approached the house, then set my partial sack of cotton where I had stopped picking. I motioned to Robert that I was heading around the barn so I could peer around the corner and see the house. He nodded and disappeared.

By the time I got to the side of the barn, Robert was there and he whispered, "It's not Margaret, but she might of hired him. Looks like a killer. Two guns and he has packages. Wonder if this is it, or if he's just acting kindly and assessing the situation."

"Why bring gifts? That's what's had me baffled."

Robert whispered, "As long as they stay outside and talk, we'll stay put. They move inside and we move in."

We waited and watched as the rider handed a package to the boy and then to Mrs. Jackson. They spoke for a bit, then the rider mounted and headed out. Robert went for the barn and I snuck back to the cotton field and went back to picking.

Mr. Jackson soon joined me, and I had to know, so I laughed. "Who was that? Santa Claus? Looked like he had packages on that horse."

"Said he was one of Margaret Sexton's men. Name is Harris. Came here to make sure you were working out. Said he'd check in again tomorrow to see if we needed any help getting this cotton to town. I told him to come for mid-afternoon meal and we'd see. Ms. Sexton sent the gifts to us as thanks for employing you out here. Harris said Ms. Sexton would like you to come to town tomorrow afternoon, sign a few papers and get a big meal at the halfway house before another day under the sun." He laughed. "I doubt you're used to this kinda work. I bet you're more used to sitting on a horse and chasin' cattle."

I laughed. "That's what I was raised up to do, but work is lean and money is leaner."

"I'll have a few easier chores for you once this cotton gets to the gin. How's that sound?"

"Much obliged." I accepted his proffered hand and hoped if we all made it through this, that I'd be able to find an honest man to take my place. I didn't think I'd last long tending crops, listening to crows and making the much-needed repairs the barn appeared to require.

Robert and I discussed my trip to town and we decided I should head out as planned, but find a place with a bit of cover, and watch the road for Harris to ride in for his supper with the Jacksons. I'd sneak in behind him and we'd catch him in the act. Hopefully before the act. We figured there wasn't any way for Margaret to know my absence at the halfway house was anything more than me running a bit late.

I accepted a few of Robert's pickled eggs before bedding down and thought no more about Margaret and her supposed thirst for blood money.

The next morning, Robert was awake before me. He kicked my booted feet and told me he was going to check on his horse he'd left by a little creek in a copse of trees about a quarter mile out. He'd be back before I headed to the cotton field for the day.

After washing up at the tank, I waited a few more minutes for Robert's return. I was a bit worried he wasn't back yet. To my relief, I spied him in the distance. He'd be in the barn before Mr. Jackson would see him. I pretended to stretch and made a small gesture so Robert would know I'd seen him. He waved and disappeared among the corn and the seemingly ineffective scarecrows in the field beside the cotton. The crows spied him and blackened the sky, then settled back to their ravenous behavior.

Mr. Jackson provided a few biscuits and salt ham for my breakfast and I downed them, then went back to picking cotton. I picked a row beside Mr. Jackson for a bit, then asked. "Not to be nosey, well maybe, but what gifts did Mrs. Sexton send to you?"

Mr. Jackson took a rare break from picking and stood straight, then leaned back – probably to get a kink out of his back. "She sent dishware for the Mrs. and a few books for Junior. I guess she knows I can't spare him much for schooling until the mortgage is paid off. The books should help him get prepared."

"Sound like great gifts. She seems to have a big heart when it comes to helping people." I waited to see if he had a response before I turned my attention back to the splayed cotton bolls.

"I hear tell she's a shrewd business woman, but I've never seen that side of her. Always helping others at any cost, is how I see it." He bent over and plucked more cotton for his sack.

I left it at that.

When the sun got to about at high as it could before descending the western sky, I figured it was time for my supposed trip to see Margaret Sexton. I was apprehensive about all this. I wasn't so sure I should wander too far from the Jackson place just in case the gift bearer was somewhere close by.

In the barn, I threw my saddle on my horse and snugged the cinch while I quietly spoke with Robert who was hidden behind the corn husks. "You sure I should head in? Feels like a trap. Maybe they know you're here. Or is this trip to town because the job doesn't lend a chance I'd be out on the range and out of touch with the happenings around here?"

"I've been thinking on that. I think we should let the Jacksons in on this. I have a plan. Go get the Jacksons and bring them in and I'll explain. I think it's the best way for all concerned, and to catch a killer."

Robert looked to the doorway and must have spied a shadow. He ducked behind the corn husks just as Mr. Jackson came in to see me off. "You have a good ride and a good meal."

"Thank you, sir, but I think we need to speak with the three of you before I head out."

"Who's we?"

"First, let me say, I'm a bounty hunter. My friend hiding behind the cornhusks is an Arizona Ranger." Robert came from behind the husks. "This is Captain Robert Fitzsimmons."

After a brief explanation, Mr. Jackson brought Mrs. and Junior out to the barn to hear the plan Robert had devised.

The plan Robert had conjured had me leaving just a bit later than planned, and since we weren't sure if the request Margaret had made was a ruse, I headed to town. I went about a mile, and stopped dead in my tracks and had a conversation with myself. "This isn't right. How can Margaret pin a murder on me if I've been seen in town at the same time the murder took place?" I rode in to a copse of mesquite and pondered. It would only take me an hour to get to town and back, so if Harris wasn't going to the ranch until a little before suppertime, he probably wouldn't leave town until he knew I was there. I smiled. I went back to the road and meandered into town, watching for trouble along the way.

The halfway house was about midway into town and I wasn't sure if someone might be able to head out of town while I was meeting with Margaret. I kept checking behind me, but didn't see anything or anybody of concern.

Margaret Sexton was sitting in a rocker on the boardwalk in front of the halfway house. She stood as I rode up. "What's wrong, Travis?"

"Not a thing, ma'am. You sent for me and here I am." I smiled, then caught confusion and urgency cross her face.

"Oh, no! Not again!"

"What, ma'am?" Now I was the one donning confusion.

"Ride, Travis! Get back to the Jackson's. They may be in trouble!"

Still confused and not knowing whether to believe her concern, I figured the best way to prevent a tragedy was to hightail it to the Jacksons, hope I wasn't riding into an ambush, and pray that Robert had things under control.

I met no resistance on the way back to the Jackson farm and was within a quarter mile of the ranch when gunfire erupted from the approximate location of the Jackson's house. I coaxed my mount, got the right response and was going through the front gate, alerting the crows who took to a raucous flight. Just as the Harris fellow stumbled backward out of the front door and landed on the front stoop, with gun still in hand, I rode up and was on top of him before he could sort the situation.

Robert peered out the door and with the barrel of his revolver, pushed his hat off his brow. "About time you showed."

"Got hungry. Is that fried chicken I smell?" I smiled and pointed at Harris. "How 'bout we tie this one up and talk this over while we eat?"

"Mr. and Mrs. are still in the barn with Junior."

I peered into the opened door and had to laugh. Robert's plan had worked.

One of the scarecrows we'd procured from the cornfield was dress as Mrs. Jackson. Another scarecrow was dressed as Mr. Jackson, and yet another was cut down to size and dressed like Junior.

I laughed again. "I guess maybe those scarecrows finally found their caw-caw calling. So, which one fried the chicken?"

"My mother's recipe. He pointed to the scarecrows. I learned a lot about cooking from my mother, and the proper way to dress from my father. Never thought I'd need to dress a scarecrow, but...."

Robert, myself and the Jacksons hauled those scarecrows back to the cornfield and they immediately went back to their mundane lives of ineffectually dissuading the crows from eating the profits.

Just before we were about to sit down to a pleasing meal of Robert's fried chicken, Mrs. Jackson's mashed potatoes, a huge bowl of green beans cooked in some of that salt ham they seemed to have in abundance, and sourdough biscuits, Margaret Sexton pulled up to the front porch in a one-horse carriage. Relief crossed her face when Mr. Jackson opened the door and all five of us stepped out onto the stoop to greet her.

Margaret had tears in her eyes as she hugged each of the Jacksons, shook my hand and stared up at Robert.

Robert offered his hand. "Captain Robert Fitzsimmons, Arizona Rangers, ma'am."

Mr. Jackson opened the door and held it for Margaret. "Come in and eat, and then we'll figure this out."

I ate my fill, waited for the others to do the same, then asked, "Okay, anybody have a clue about what just happened here?"

Margaret wiped her mouth on a napkin. "Do you have the murderer?"

Once Margaret had a good look at the man we had bound, gagged and tied to a post at the edge of the cornfield not far from the redeemed scarecrows, it didn't take too long to put it all together. Margaret explained her short stint at banking up in Denver. Seems she wasn't the one stealing the money, but took the fall for her then fiancé, the bank manager, Max Harris.

When the Bank of Denver noticed, once again, that a large amount of money was unaccounted for, they hired a Pinkerton to investigate. Max Harris was caught red-handed and given jailtime. He escaped on the way to Yuma Territorial Prison and hadn't been seen again, until now.

Margaret sighed. "I don't know what I was thinking, covering for Max like I did. I guess I was in love and knew Daddy would help me so I wouldn't go to prison. I had big plans for Max and me, but as soon as Daddy bailed me out, Max broke the engagement. He said a bank manager couldn't be seen with a thief. I was so embarrassed that I could be used like that. I told everyone I was the one who ended the relationship.

"About a year ago, I received a letter from Max. I never told anyone but Lizbeth. I swore her to secrecy. Max said he was sorry, he missed me, and he had come up with a plan to pay Daddy back all the money. I never would have had anything more to do with him, but there wasn't a return address, so I couldn't say my piece.

"After the Odoms were slain, I started to wondering if Max was behind the other two murders. I wondered if the foreclosure and reselling the properties was his plan for getting money back in Daddy's pocket, but I couldn't believe he'd go from thief to murderer. I guess I should have shared my concern with someone beside Lizbeth. The Odoms were such a nice family, and those little ones...." Margaret wiped a tear from her cheek, sat back and asked. "So how did you catch him?"

Robert explained, "Travis and I couldn't rule out you as an accomplice since you employed the drifters and would stand to capitalize on the resale of the Odom place and the previous ones." Robert sighed. "Sorry, Margaret, but we had to be sure and you've just provided the proof we needed.

"The Jacksons, along with Travis, brought in three of the five scarecrows from out in the cornfield. We figured it was time they earn their keep. I snuck in the back way and helped Mrs. Jackson dress them up so they'd look real enough for the murderer to be fooled. Once the scarecrows were in place, the Jacksons snuck to the barn to be out of harm's way.

"It's hard to pull anything over on that bunch of crows. They seem to know everything that goes on around here. But that helped me to know someone was approaching.

"I really didn't expect them so soon, but when I heard the crows, I knew it had to be the suspect — you or someone who knew your business. Sounds like you alerted Travis to a problem just in time for him to get back here and act like he was the hero." Robert laughed. "I guess he did help, if just a bit."

I sat back and crossed my arms. "But what's with the gifts?"

Margaret sighed, "I think it was to set me up to take another fall for his crimes, just in case the drifter – as my workers are sometimes known – had an alibi or could prove innocence in some way. Those gifts would help to put that noose a bit tighter around my neck."

"How so?"

"For several years, I've been buying Mother's Oats for myself and then I continued to buy it once I started the halfway house. We go through a lot of oatmeal and it always comes with free dishware. We can't use all of it at the halfway house, so I give it to families who needed it after their stay at the house. It's not much, but it means a lot to a family who's lost everything during this depression. It gives them something to start their new home with. And the books? I always have books and toys for the children who spend time at the halfway house. Children need something besides work and worry. So again, the families who have stayed with us take books with them when they leave. It's never too early, or late, to learn to appreciate books.

"Even if I wasn't the one who pulled the trigger, they could get me for conspiracy to commit murder. I'm sure Max had something in place to allude to me hiring someone to do the killing."

I sighed, "Well, we might never know the whole story if Max doesn't tell us, but at least we have him. There are two other Arizona Rangers who will meet us here tomorrow. They should have proof on Harris' involvement with the other murders and his procurement of dishware and books. And to believe, Margaret, you were almost framed by a book, some crayons and free dishware from a box of oatmeal." I shook my head and laughed. "Let's get that murderer to town, send a telegram to your father and get the trial over and done with so Robert and I can witness justice and be on our way to the next assignment. Can't believe it took a murder of crows to help catch a murderer."

Beauty and the Bounty Hunter

A Travis Cooper Tail

After a leisurely breakfast at Café Bonita in the small railroad town of Benson, Arizona, and a stroll on the boardwalk, Arizona Ranger Captain Robert Fitzsimmons stepped from the telegraph office, looked up at the morning sun, then pulled his hat a bit lower to shade his eyes. Yesterday, he'd sent a telegram – asking for help – to a friend. He was surprised when the telegrapher hailed him and gestured for him to come into the office, then handed him a telegram. Captain Fitzsimmons hadn't expected an answer so soon. He read the message: *TC the Kid 5 p.m. tomorrow.* He'd chuckled. "Damn kid is crazy. I'd better get on down to Elfrida and see if I can round up any more information about this bandit."

The next evening, at exactly five o'clock, bounty hunter Travis Cooper stepped from the train, retrieved his horse and saddle from the stock car, took them to the livery, then walked directly to the sheriff's office. Now, working toward eighteen, Travis, still baby-faced, was tall, lanky and full of vinegar, but had proven himself to be quite helpful in several of Captain Fitzsimmons' recent investigations and apprehensions as well as a few of his own.

Sheriff Joe McLeod stood from his desk and offered his hand. Travis accepted McLeod's proffered hand and glanced around the small office. "You're lookin' right fit, Sheriff. Where's Robert?"

"He's getting a little more information about this bandit from the ranchers down near ElFrida. He should be back by noon tomorrow."

"What are we lookin' at, so far?"

"Have a seat and I'll get you a cup of coffee."

Travis parked his lanky frame in a chair beside the sheriff's desk. He glanced around the small office. "Got a few handbills up there that were here the last time I visited." He nodded when Sheriff McLeod pointed to the cream pitcher, then commented on the yellowed wanted posters. "Are you usin' them for decoration, or are those men still available for a sizeable paycheck?"

McLeod laughed as he placed a mug of heavily-creamed coffee on the desk in front of Travis and another on his side of the desk. "They're still out there."

Travis took a sip of coffee, grimaced, set the cup on the desk, pushed the toxic brew away and sat back. "And what kinda bandit are we lookin' at this time?"

Sheriff McLeod chuckled. "Coffee a bit harsh?"

"Not if I'm needin' it to kill varmints." He shifted in his seat. "Now, back to the task at hand. Tell me about this bandit."

"Rides in like he's injured. Yells for help, or falls off his horse in front of the target's house, then moans like he's dying. The husbands are always out on the range when this happens, so the wife helps the man inside to care for him. Before she knows it, he's got a gun on her and demands food and money."

Travis removed his hat, rubbed his forehead with the back of his hand, replace his hat and said, "He'd do more than moan if the wife fed him some of your coffee." He shook his head. "And who around here has any money just layin' around?"

McLeod chuckled. "Show's how intelligent he is. I guess he'll keep fallin' off horses until he figures out who does have money." McLeod shook his head. "He's never seriously hurt anyone and he always asks politely. The Gentleman Bandit is what he's being called."

"What would happen if they didn't give him any money?"

"Some don't. As you pointed out, who around here has any? But most have provisions. And I guess he figures a few days' worth of food gives him a full belly and time to find a new target."

"Don't you have a description? Can't anyone identify him?"

McLeod pointed to the wall full of wanted posters. "They've all pointed to that handbill on the top left. We know who he is. Wilber Banks. We just haven't caught him. He's as wily as a coyote and as elusive as a gila monster. He's been known to pull this stunt from

Tucson to Tombstone, and possibly Willcox to Safford. Since his thieving started, nobody but the victims have ever seen him. A man from down around Bisbee came in one day, saw that handbill and said he knew him from around Steins over in New Mexico Territory. Used to mine ore with him. That's how we put a name to the face."

Travis shook his head. "And no one's the wiser about his particular habits? Or, maybe just not particularly concerned." He crossed his arms, thought a moment, then resumed his assumptions. "I suppose the women all turn motherly when he plops off his horse and moans. Hell, if he's not hurting anyone, the women might feel they've done their Christian duty by providing food, and sometimes a bit of money for the downtrodden." Travis laughed. "I think I have an idea, but we'll wait for Robert. How about supper at the hotel? You eaten yet?"

"I was waiting on you. Milly, the missus, is working on supper. Should be done by the time we get there. You don't need a hotel room. Milly has the guest room ready."

"Thank you for the room tonight, but it might be smarter for me to stay at the hotel after that. If Wilber Banks happens into town, it won't appear that I'm associated with you. And the hotel will fit into a plan I'm hatchin' as we speak." Travis chuckled.

"I doubt we'll see him in town unless he's bein' escorted by a rancher or the law." McLeod glanced at the clock on the wall. "It's about that time. Let's head over for supper."

"Milly, this is Travis Cooper, Robert's friend and cohort."

Travis removed his hat and noticed that while Sheriff McLeod was almost as tall as him, Mrs. McLeod wasn't far from it, and quite a handsome woman. "Good evening. I hope this isn't an imposition."

She waved a hand at him. "Nonsense. Any friend, *or cohort* of Joe or Robert, is always welcome in our home. Come sit. Supper is almost ready."

Travis took a seat at an oval table in the well-appointed dining room. He hung his hat on the back of the chair as Joe set a small glass in front of him and held up a bottle. "A little cider while we wait?"

Travis grinned. “Won’t say no. Wouldn’t be polite.”

Joe poured some of the golden liquid into Travis’ glass, then filled his own. He took his place at the table and raised his glass. “To catching the Gentleman Bandit.”

Travis raised his glass and tapped it against Joe’s. “To catching the Gentleman Bandit.”

Milly entered with a tray of pan-fried chops and potatoes and placed them on the table. “Dig in. I know you must be starved after your train ride. I’ll be back with more.”

The men where heaping food on their plates when Milly entered again. This time she set down a plate of biscuits and a bowl of butter beans, then took her place opposite her husband. “I have rhubarb pie for dessert, so save room.”

With little conversation, the three of them ate heartily. Not used to being around women, Travis enjoyed watching Milly’s feminine mannerisms as she ate. Joe was the first to clean his plate. He moved it to the side and offered each of them a glass of brandy to go with dessert. Milly nodded and excused herself to bring in the pie while Joe poured the brandy.

Travis finished his dessert and patted his stomach. “That was excellent, Ma’am. Thank you.” He waited patiently for the couple to finish up, then helped Milly clear the table. Not used to the habits of women of societal means, he considered her gestures as she spoke.

“Thank you for your help, Travis. You and Joe have a seat in the parlor. I’m going to clean up and head upstairs for the night. Joe will show you to your room when you’re ready.”

Travis woke to the aroma of coffee, bacon and eggs. He sat up in bed and took another whiff. *And more of those tasty biscuits! Beats the hell outta cold, canned sausage and stale corn dodgers*. He dressed quickly, took advantage of the chamber pot, then met Joe in the upstairs hallway. Joe led the way down the steps. Milly called from the kitchen. “Sit yourselves down. Coffee is on the table. Breakfast is coming up.”

All through breakfast, Travis continued to watch Milly, enjoying her prim habits and noted just a touch of endearing southern drawl in her speech.

Once again, Travis helped to clear the table. He thanked Milly, praised her coffee, then shook hands with Joe. "I'd better get over and get a room before the two o'clock stage hits town and the hotel fills up. Do you know if Robert already has a room?"

"I've reserved room three for him. Said he'd be back from Elfrida by noon."

"Let's say we meet up again at the hotel dining room around two. That gives him time to get all spiffy again." Travis chuckled." You know how he hates to look like he just came off the trail." Travis jutted his chin. "Does that work for you?"

McLeod tilted his head to one side. "Should you be seen with the two of us?"

Travis laughed. "After careful consideration, it doesn't sound like our miscreant would chance being seen in town, so I don't think that will be an issue."

Travis procured a room down the hall from Robert's, then did a bit of shopping. He had what he thought was a great plan, but needed a few accoutrements from the local stores. Once he returned to his room, he opened the largest package and admired it. He opened several smaller packages and set them on the dresser. He'd get everything in order so he could see what Robert and Joe had to say about his idea for catching the Gentleman Bandit.

Just a little before noon, Captain Robert Fitzsimmons rode up to the front of the hotel. He tied his horse to the rail and climbed the three steps to the boardwalk. One old cat stretched and yawned from beneath a bench as Robert approached. The elderly man in the seat closest to the doorway nodded a greeting to him. The fashionable young woman in the rocker on the other side of the doorway never looked up, seemingly enthralled with the book she appeared to be reading.

Robert entered the hotel and proceeded to the counter. "Hey, Tony. Could I have a tub of clean, hot water ready for me in about twenty minutes?"

"Sure thing, Captain Fitzsimmons. No one else in the wash room, so you'll have it all to yourself. Sheriff has room three reserved for you."

Robert tipped his hat. "Thanks, Tony. Have you seen Travis?"

"Sure did. He said he'd meet you and Sheriff McLeod in the dining room around two." Tony nodded and smiled. "Made the reservation myself."

Just before two o'clock, Sheriff McLeod entered the hotel. He spied Robert seated near the center of the dining room. Coffee was already on the table. He laughed as he sat.

Robert furrowed his brow. "What's so funny?"

"Travis said you'd need time to spiff up before dinner." He whiffed the air. "Looks, *and smells*, like he's got you pegged."

Robert laughed. "That he does." Robert glanced around the room. He smiled and nodded to the young lady two tables over, who had previously occupied the rocking chair in front of the hotel, then turned his attention back to Sheriff McLeod. "Speaking of Travis, why isn't he here? He's usually right on time."

"He was the one who said two o'clock. Maybe he fell asleep. If he's not here in a few minutes, I'll send Tony up to knock on his door. Stage was outside, so Tony's probably checking in all the passengers. He'll be over in a few minutes to take our orders." McLeod noticed that the young woman two tables over appeared to be staring at Robert. He smiled and tipped his hat. He leaned toward Robert. "I think that young women just might be enamored with you. Maybe we should ask her to join us. Uh, oh. No need." He shifted his focus to the table cloth and drummed his fingers, then glanced toward the woman. "Here she comes. Walks like she comes from money. Prim and proper... and mighty sure of herself. Do you want to ask her to join us?"

"I suppose it would be the gentlemanly thing to do." Robert stood, as did Joe. When Robert turned to face the lady, he did everything in his power to control his emotions. He held out a seat for her and she accepted.

She adjusted her bonnet and shawl, then sat, as did the men. She placed her hands in her lap and in a southern draw said, "Well, good afternoon, gentleman. Whom do I have the pleasure of meetin' on this fine day?"

Joe took a sip of coffee, but upon assessing the young lady, swallowed and choked. His eyes began to water as he tried to regain his composure.

Robert laughed quietly, then said, "I think you've made a real impression on my friend. He's usually more adept at drinking coffee in front of beautiful ladies."

"Why, thank you for that explanation. I was concerned I'd made an enemy my first day in this charmin' little town. I hope he'll recover. I see he has a badge. I'd like a word with him in his office around four. Would that be possible?"

Joe gained control of himself and nodded. "That works for me. Would you like Captain Fitzsimmons to join us?"

The lady turned to Robert as she smoothed her skirt. "And what, pray tell, would you be a captain of?"

Robert grinned. "The Arizona Rangers, Miss."

"Very well. You may join us, but for now, I'll leave the two of you to your coffee." She winked at Joe. "I hope the rest of it goes down more smoothly." She turned to leave, then over her shoulder she remarked in a rather loud voice, "Oh, my name is Poppy Wells. Heiress of a small gold mine up near Jerome. I just purchased the old Davis ranch down near Elfrida. Hope to raise some cattle. Maybe I'll see all y'all around." She sashayed across the dining room and up the stairway, leaving Joe and Robert shaking their heads.

Joe raised his brow. "Now, that was something!"

Robert chuckled, "Indeed it was. Don't see women like that very often."

Tony came out from behind the front desk. "I got busy with the passengers on the stage and couldn't get away to let you know that Travis stopped by while you were takin' a bath and told me to tell you he'd be a little late for your meeting. Should be here by two-thirty."

Robert nodded. "Can you bring us three menus and beer? I think we're gonna need it."

When Travis joined McLeod and Robert, he laid out his plan, then asked, "Well, what do you think?"

McLeod leaned back in his chair and tapped his fingers on the table. "So... that's your plan?"

"Why, yes. It is."

"Well, don't that beat the fuzz off a peach. I'm thinking you might be good at planning. Where'd you get the idea."

"I've kept my eyes open for who the likely targets might be, and Poppy Wells just seemed to appear out of nowhere. I think she'll be a fine bait."

"So, you think Poppy Wells is the answer to catching this miscreant?"

Travis grinned. "That, I do. She's rich, appears to be traveling alone. I think if word gets around, she'll be a target for the Gentlemen Bandit. We just need to set the trap to grab him before he has a chance to do Poppy any harm." Travis shook his head. "Just 'cause he's been a gentleman so far, doesn't mean it'll hold up once he gets a chance at a woman the likes of Poppy Wells." He knitted his brow. "Now, of course, we should make sure Poppy doesn't mind bein' bait." He smiled. "I just encountered her briefly, but I think you have to admit she fits the bill. I'll interact with her again, and hopefully, she'll be on board with all of this."

Robert chuckled. "I think she'll listened to you. How about you, *and Poppy,* hash this out and you meet us here for breakfast in the morning. If all goes well, we'll start spreading a rumor about our heiress."

Sheriff McLeod grinned and nodded. "And I know just how to get it started."

With Poppy Wells on board, Sheriff McLeod placed the rumor into the mill and smiled as the cogs started to grind in the head of the man who had been standing behind him. He then went to meet Robert and Travis for dinner at the hotel.

McLeod laughed as he explained to Robert and Travis. "I had the missus accompany me to the mercantile this morning, and with her blessing, we put the tale in motion. Seems Lyle Walthers is always leaning into other people's business and he's always stocking shelves at the mercantile first thing in the morning. The missus picked up an outlandishly flowered hat, as we had planned. Being it isn't her usual style, Lyle moved to a ladder on the shelves behind us, most likely to see if he could find out the occasion for such a purchase. Well, I started telling the missus about Poppy Wells, her inheritance and the ranch she had purchased. I also mentioned I was worried about a woman like Poppy, with no man for protection, being so far from town." He chuckled. "Lyle almost fell off the ladder when I said that. He'll have told enough people about her that within twenty-four hours, everyone from here up to Phoenix and down to Bisbee will know about Miss Poppy Wells and her fortune."

Travis grinned. "I guess Robert and me better get Poppy and ride south and set up at the old Davis place. We'll be ready when the Gentleman Bandit shows his face."

Robert chuckled. "Do you need a little extra time to clean up? Or are you going just as you are?"

Travis looked down at his well-worn dungarees and faded brown cotton shirt. "I'll ride just as I am." He chuckled and clapped Robert on the shoulder. "Wouldn't want anyone spreading rumors about you and me." He grinned. "And Poppy likes me just the way I am."

Several hours later, Robert and Travis opened the sagging barn door at the run-down Davis ranch. "All right, Travis, I'll get set up in here while you get Poppy situated in the ranch house. I hope she's not afraid of spiders and snakes. That front door was wide open."

"Spiders!"

"Yep. You know, those eight-legged, web-weaving critters."

Travis pulled his gun from his holster, checked it and replaced it.

Robert laughed. "I expected a Southern Belle to be a bit fearful, but I didn't think you'd bat an eye over a few creepy-crawling, egg-sac-hanging, web-weaving, fly-eating spiders." He pointed to the gun in Travis' hand. "And that gun is a bit of an overkill."

Travis shivered. "I don't like spiders, and I'll venture that Poppy will agree. You wanna find a weapon of some kind and clear 'em out for me?"

"I suppose I could help with that, since you're here to help me."

"Much appreciated. And I'm sure Poppy will be thankful for not having a bunch of creepy-crawlies in her bloomers!"

Spiders and other critters expelled from the old ranch house, Travis entered and set up a web of his own. He went to the back room and a few moments later, with more confidence about the plan and thankful for a web-free abode, Poppy Wells walked into the dilapidated kitchen, grabbed an old rag from the sink and wiped two years of old dust and bird poop from a cane-bottom chair, then sat and waited.

As darkness approached, Robert came in to check on her. Poppy went to the back room, procured a bottle from the saddle bag that lay on the bedsprings, brought it out and grabbed two chipped cups from the shelf above the sink. She curtsied, smiled and in a southern drawl she asked, "May I pour you a drink, Captain Fitzsimmons? Whiskey always helps to pass the time and I understand our bandit doesn't stray after nightfall."

Robert laughed. "Why, Miss Poppy, I thought you'd never ask. And I agree. I think we're safe until morning. I'll have that drink, and then let you get some sleep. I'll retreat to the barn, just in case our bandit changes his habits and shows up before daylight. I'm sure Travis will keep you safe in here."

"I've come to realize just how handsome and courageous our Travis is. Why, I'd trust him to protect me to the ends of the earth! I've never met a man so wonderful as Travis. Sorry if I go on about him, but a little voice inside of me just thinks you need to hear it."

Robert shook his head and grinned. "I'll bet it does." He gulped down the contents of the cup and excused himself, laughing all the way to the barn.

The following day, it was well past noon when Robert spied a cloud of dust on the lane leading to the old ranch house. He threw an old corn cob toward the house, and when it fell short, he tried again. He knew his second try had succeeded when the door squealed on its rusted hinges and Poppy appeared in the doorway. She glanced toward the hayloft, and then in the direction Robert was pointing. She nodded, closed the door, and prepared herself for what was to follow.

Twenty minutes passed as she waited for the cry of a man in distress. And then she heard him.

"Help! Oh, my! Is anyone home? My horse threw me a ways back, but I was able to get back on. But, if I try to get off by myself, I fear I'll be further injured. Can someone help me?"

Poppy threw open the door and started toward the supposedly injured man. She glanced toward the barn to make sure Robert was ready to intervene, and as she did, she tripped on a broken step and landed face down in the dirt at the horse's hooves. She stood to brush herself off, but when she did, her bloomers fell to her dusty boot tops, a blonde wig fell to the ground and the strings on a too-tight corset broke loose and several woolen socks tumbled out of their confines, exposing a hairy, unencumbered chest.

The Gentleman Bandit took one surprised look at the man disguised as a woman and turned his horse to ride away. As Robert grabbed the reins to stop the bandit, Travis pulled his lacy bloomers back in place, regained control of his remaining feminine garments, pulled the bandit from the saddle, and in a southern-belle accent said, "Mr.! I think you've ruined my reputation!"

With the Gentleman Bandit behind bars, Sheriff McLeod poured a stiff drink for Robert, Travis and himself. He took his seat behind his desk and chuckled. "Well, I'll be damned. It worked."

Travis, in his now perfected southern-belle voice, batted his eyes and said, "Why, Sheriff, how could you ever doubt me? I'm a real beauty of a bounty hunter when I have to be."

Robert set a jar on the desk. The large eight-legged creature within, circled the bottom of the jar. Travis jumped up from his chair, toppling it, and ran for the door. Robert laughed. "Yep. He's a real beauty all right. And a fast one, at that."

Salted and Hornswoggled

A Travis Cooper Tale

Travis Cooper, chin up and standing tall, laughed as he spoke with Big Joe Wilder. "I can't believe he give up so easy. Yella-belly is what he was. He'll live to tell about it, but I don't think he'll tell the whole tale."

Big Joe slapped Travis on the back. "That was a real piece of thinkin', Trav. Don't believe they'll look for us here. That rain will cover our tracks so they won't be on our trail real soon, anyhow. We'll rest up, then divide this ore. Keep some of it hidden 'til we can get back and cover the rest with them Mexican blankets like we was honest folk takin' a load of goods to market." He laughed. "I guess we gotta figure out who's gonna drive this wagon to Millville."

"Well, Big Joe, everybody knows you, and most know Willie, Claude and Smiley. Maybe I oughta be the driver. A few might recognize me, but I'll use my feminine wiles, just like I done on that wagon master." Travis shook his head as he chuckled. "Shame you couldn't see the look on his face when he stopped that wagon for a damsel in a soaked dress and ended up with a .45 in his face. I knew that downpour would help my disguise. Dress got all clingy..." Travis put his hands on his chest. "...and them coyote melons I had in my corset helped ensure my endowments would stop any man in his tracks."

Big Joe supervised as Travis and his crew of three, unloaded most of the ore and covered it with mud and sticks. He chuckled when Travis used a bit of a vine and fashioned a cross from two large sticks and stuck them into the muddy mound.

Travis pushed his hat from his brow, stood back, crossed his arms and laughed. "Doubt anybody'd wanna dig up a corpse."

Big Joe chortled. “You got a real good head for thievin’, Trav. Glad to have you on my crew. Them other three ain’t much good for thinkin’. I’m kinda wore out from doin’ all the plannin’ on my own.”

Travis nodded. “Pleasure workin’ with you, Big Joe. Got kinda wore out myself. But my wore out was from upholdin’ the law and stayin’ broke when I could be breakin’ the law and gettin’ rich.”

Big Joe puffed out his chest and raised his brow. “You gotta admit, it’s easier to thieve than to work.”

“Sure is. Don’t know why I ever took to bein’ law abidin’, ‘cept to get help from that ranger for catchin’ them that killed my father.” Travis stuck his thumbs in his pockets and chuckled. “Sure had him hornswoggled.”

Big Joe turned to the rest of his crew and spun a finger in the air. “Let’s wrap it up boys. We’ll go on into Contention and have us a celebratory beer.”

Travis put one hand beside his mouth and got close to Big Joe’s ear. “If’n you don’t mind, I got a girl in Tombstone I’d like to visit.”

“Go on then, get them knots out so you can be here to take them *blankets* to Millville.” Wilder winked.

Travis knitted his brow when the jail cell door clanged shut. He stuck his arms through uprights and rested them on the crossbar. “I don’t see why you won’t send that telegram. I’m sure Robert could clear me of all this.”

White looked him in the eye. “Not gonna happen.” He shook his head. “If you hadn’t noticed, you’re on the wrong side of the bars to be askin’ for favors, kid.”

Travis stood away from the bars and crossed his arms in front of his chest. “Can I ask? Why did you arrest me?”

“You were seen in a saloon in Contention talkin’ with Big Joe Wilder and his gang a day or so ago.”

Travis kept his stance. “I didn’t think havin’ a beer with a fella was against the law.”

White, chest out, stood tall. “According to an eye witness, you were seen riding out with him. Nobody rides with Big Joe Wilder unless they’re in cahoots with him.”

Travis relaxed his stance and sighed. “Could you please send a telegram to Robert? He should be in Benson, but you might put it over the wire to Bisbee, too. I think he had business in both places this week. Don’t mention my name. Just tell him he’s needed.”

Marshal White huffed. “I’ll think on it.” He strutted out the door and took up a seat on the bench by the jailhouse window.

Deputy Cross strolled down the boardwalk, took one look at Marshal White, and put his hands on his hips. “That’s a mighty big scowl you got all over your face, Marshal. What’s eatin’ at you?”

“I knew that kid would turn bad. You can’t have a rustler for a father and not pick up bad habits.”

Cross tipped his head to one side. “Who’s that, Marshal?”

“Travis Cooper! He pretends to be a good kid. Got the captain of the Arizona Rangers to believe in him just long enough to solve a few crimes and retaliate against the gang that killed his rustler father.” He slammed his fist on his knee and shook his head. “But I knew… I just knew.”

“What’d he do to get you so dad-blasted riled?”

“Joined the Wilder gang. I bet he was in on that shipment that got robbed just this mornin’. A wagon full of Tombstone ore on its way to Millville.”

“Dad-gum if that ain’t a first! We ain’t never lost a shipment!”

“Well, we can’t say that now, can we?”

“What are we gonna do about it? We’re a rough town, right now. Can’t see a way of mindin’ Tombstone and followin’ ore thieves at the same time.”

“We’ll put out word to be on the lookout for Big Joe Wilder and his bunch. He might figure they’ll hide the ore and get shut of Tombstone and Millville for a spell.”

Cross tilted his head to the other side. “I ‘spose that would be an idea.”

That afternoon, Arizona Ranger Captain Robert Fitzsimmons received a telegram from a friend in Tombstone telling him about an ore shipment heist and that a friend of his had been arrested. Fitzsimmons was soon on his way.

Once in Tombstone, Captain Fitzsimmons checked into the Russ House on Fifth and asked the desk clerk for hot water for a bath. Refreshed and in clean clothes, he headed to the Oriental to see if there were any rumors about the robbery. Everyone was talking about the hold-up, but no one had any details other than it being Big Joe Wilder and his crew... and Travis Cooper.

White watched as Fitzsimmons tied his horse to the rail, then met him at the door and gestured for the ranger to stay on the boardwalk.

"You've got to trust him, Sheriff." Robert shook his head as he brushed mud from his pant leg. "I think I know what he's got going and he figured I'd be alerted to the problem. We have a history, that kid and me."

Marshal White, his brow furrowed, shook his head. "I don't know about you bein' involved in this, Captain. Might look like you're part of it. You've got your reputation to consider."

"What other information do you have? Anything about how they stopped that wagon? Or where they stopped it?" Robert moved toward the jail house window. He peered in.

White put up one hand. "You don't need to see him just yet. You see if you can get any information to change my mind about his intentions, then you can see him... for a minute." White moved to get it front of the window. "Got it stopped just shy of Millville. Mitch, the wagon master, said there was something laying in the road. Nobody has been out to check the scene. As much as it was raining, I doubt they'll be any trail to follow. I've sent telegrams to all the nearby towns to be on the lookout for Big Joe's gang."

"How'd Mitch get back to town?"

"Frank Watts was headin' in from Contention. Found Mitch tied to a tree."

"And Watts didn't see anyone else anywhere on the road?"

"Only one he saw was Mike Downs. He came up behind Frank while he was cuttin' the rope to get Mitch shut of that tree. I spoke with Mike and he didn't see anyone else besides Frank and Mitch."

"If you hear anything, I've got a room at the Russ House. I doubt Big Joe would be dumb enough to come to Tombstone, and he might not know you've got the kid." Robert sighed. "If you don't trust Travis, could you at least put a little faith in me? Would you let me speak with Travis, in private?"

Marshal White waited on the boardwalk. A few minutes later, Fitzsimmons led Travis out of the jailhouse. "He's still cuffed, but I'm taking him. He'll be my responsibility."

White shook his head. "I don't like it, but it's all on you, now. And I don't think you know what you're getttin' yourself into, Captain."

"I have a pretty good idea, and Travis can clear up anything I can't figure out."

Once Fitzsimmons had Travis alone, he removed the cuffs and they discussed the stolen shipment of ore.

"I've got it all figured, Robert. Just need to get back before Big Joe starts to miss me too much. I lied and told him I had a girl here in Tombstone. Came to town to send you a telegram. White got me before I could send it. I didn't trust the telegraphers in those other towns. Big Joe seems to have influence over a lot of people up that way."

"I'm sure White had your horse taken to the livery." Robert checked their surroundings. "Go through the alley. I don't want White stopping you again. I'll do some asking around and you make sure I can find you again. I'm going to find the wagon master and ask him some questions. Anything you want to tell me first?"

Travis looked at the ground and shook his head. "Nope. It won't be anything you haven't heard, *or seen*, before." He stood tall and chuckled. "Where the guy was tied to a tree, you'll find my first clue to the east of the San Pedro."

Mitch, the wagon master, took his hat off and scratched his head. "Like I told Marshal White, it was Big Joe and a new kid. Kind'a tall and scrawny, once he showed his *real* self. Heard it was a fella you might know. Travis somethin' or other. He just come out and told me his name. Kinda proud, he seemed." Mitch tapped a finger on his brow. "Cooper, that was it. Travis Cooper. So, you know him?" He shook his head. "I'll tell you what I ain't told no other. Not even Marshal White." He looked around to make sure he wouldn't be overheard. "Kid was dressed like a woman." He put his hands several inches from his chest. "Fooled me with them melons he had hid in his shirt. Took 'em right out and showed 'em to me so I'd know he was just a baby-faced kid."

"How do you know he was with Big Joe?"

"Told me right out. He whispered that Big Joe thanked me for helpin' with his income. Then he put a bag over my head and I heard some others come out from the brush and they tied me to that tree where Frank found me. Lucky that Frank come along when he did. I was gettin' chilled from all the rain and a little croaky from all my yellin'." Mitch shivered as he put his hand to his throat. "That help you any, Captain?"

Captain Robert Fitzsimmons shook Mitch's hand. "You've been a really big help, Mitch." He laughed. "And you don't have to tell White everything you told me. I've got a room at Russ House until this is sorted out. If you think of anything else, leave a message at the desk."

Fitzsimmons spoke with Sheriff White. "Where can I find this Frank who brought Mitch back to town?"

"Probably over at Big Nose, or at the Bird Cage. He comes here to drink. Seems he's had a few too many, too many times, in Contention. Got thrown out of most of those saloons for startin' fights. Seems to behave when he's here." White shook his head. "Still don't like you takin' that kid. Hope you're keepin' him in line."

Fitzsimmons checked at the Bird Cage, then Big Nose Kate's. Frank was at the bar talking to another man about finding Mitch tied to a tree. Fitzsimmons tapped him on the shoulder. "Are you the man who found Mitch?"

Frank turned and noted the ranger badge, then looked up at Robert. "Why, yes, I am. What can I do for you, Captain?"

"I need you to take me out to where you found him."

Frank downed his beer, wiped his mouth on his sleeve and tipped his hat to the man he'd been speaking with, then turned to Robert. "Might as well go now, before another storm hits."

Captain Fitzsimmons and Frank Leeds rode in silence for the better part of the way. A little less than two miles out of Millville, Frank stopped and pointed to a sycamore on the bank of the San Pedro. "Found him right there. Had a bag over his head. Didn't see him right away. Pourin' rain at the time. Heard him, though." Frank laughed. "He's got a set of lungs on him, all right!"

"If you want to head back to town, go on. I'll check the site and see if I can come up with a direction to look."

"Fine by me, Captain." Leeds touched a finger to his hat. "See you around."

Robert waited until Frank was out of sight. He urged his horse into the cool water and headed east of the San Pedro as Travis had instructed. His first clue was a coyote melon balanced in the crotch of a cholla. The second was another melon balanced in much the same manner. He found a cairn and turned in the suggested direction. He went another fifty feet and passed into a copse of scrub oak. Right in the middle was a mound of mud adorned with a cross. Robert laughed. "And just what does Big Joe Wilder think he's going to do with the bounty I'll bet is under that cross?" He shook his head. "Big Joe sure has put a lot of faith in that kid."

Big Joe's gang wasn't at the campsite, so Travis headed into Contention. He pasted on an ear-to-ear grin as he approached Big Joe. He leaned toward Big Joe and whispered. "Had me a good time in Tombstone. I surely did. That girl had me every which way." He looked around to see where the rest of the crew was. "Are we headin' back?"

"Yep. Talked with my pard up here. He'll be ready for you. Let's head south." As he spun one finger in the air, Big Joe yelled for his crew. "Get it goin', boys. You got work to do if you figure on gettin' paid."

Back at the *burial* site, Big Joe watched as his crew covered the unloaded portion of ore with blankets. "All right, Trav. Dress proper for a lady. Go north a ways on the old trail toward Benson, then turn back south and take her on into Millville by the main road. Look for Harry Long. Can't miss him." Big Joe put one hand near his waist. "Beard to here. Braided with a three gold coins for show." He chortled. "Said he shot them holes in them coins on the fly, but he'd be hard pressed to put a slug in a snake oil salesman if he was standin' an inch in front of his barrel. Hell, them coins is worth more than he'll ever make honest."

"So, how's this Harry Long figure in?"

"Says he's got a no-good mine just outside of Contention. He'll hide this wagon and move a few pounds of the ore to his wagon, salt his hole in the ground, and make like he found enough silver ore to have it stamped, then find a sucker to buy his worthless mine. He splits the profit with us, and we try it again with a little more of that ore. Harry will salt another hole in the ground and find another sucker. Done it before near Steins and in the Dragoons and will keep doin' it until all this ore is used. We make more on them salted mines than we do with the stolen ore. And tryin' to sell or stamp that ore would get us caught in a hurry." Big Joe chuckled. "Like they say, '*there's a sucker born every day.*' Them salted mines will sell quick. Good thing, too. I'd hate to have to work up a sweat for a profit." He twirled a finger in the air. "Head on out. Get it done, then steer clear of here and meet us back at camp."

Harry Long laughed at Travis' disguise and holstered his revolver. "Never woulda know'd you was a part of this if that wig hadn't a slipped a bit." Harry provided Travis with a mule to get him back to Big Joe's Camp. Travis skirted the camp and proceeded to the buried ore. He dismounted, took a stick and drew an arrow in the mud. Beside it, he wrote the number one with a plus sign beside it. He mounted and rode back to camp, removed his feminine attire, poured a cup of coffee from the pot on the fire, then settled onto a log.

One leg forward, hands on hips, and a big grin, Wilder greeted Travis. "Bet you rattled ol' Harry with that getup of yours."

"Hit a rough spot in the road and my wig slipped. Otherwise, he mighta plugged me."

Wilder chuckled. "He wouldn't have shot you, but he might have tried to bed you."

After a good night's sleep, Captain Robert Fitzsimmons dined on Nellie Cashman's biscuits and gravy, and just as the sun was rising into a clear blue sky, headed back toward Millville. He followed his previous route, checked for any new clues, and smiled when he saw what Travis had written on the mound. He turned back toward Tombstone.

"Sheriff White?"

Brow raised, White looked up from his seat at the desk. "What'd you find out?"

"I know where the gang is camped. They're just a bit shy of Millville. Haven't laid eyes on it, but I know it to be fact."

White slapped the top of his desk. "Right in my own back yard. Well, I'll be damned. Bet Big Joe is pullin' that mine saltin' trick. Can't think of any other reason to steal ore and stick so close to the source. He's been saltin' mines from here to Steins and over in the Santa Ritas. Never could prove it was him, or who was his accomplice at the stamps. Maybe you can squeeze the kid and get him to squeal."

Fitzsimmons laughed. "He'll squeal, but I don't have to squeeze."

Sheriff White rounded up a posse and followed Captain Fitzsimmons. About a half mile from the camp, Fitzsimmons stopped. He pulled a turkey call from the pocket of his jacket and smiled.

Sheriff White knitted his brow. "What in tarnation are you gonna do with that?"

"When you hear this..." He worked the turkey call. "...you go on into camp and get Big Joe and his gang. I'll take care of the kid."

White gave him a sideways stare. "I'm still not sure about that kid, but it seems like you got somethin' up your sleeve."

"We'll talk all this out when we get back to Tombstone." Fitzsimmons put the paddle shaped turkey call back in his pocket and rode quickly toward the northeast and circled around while the posse rode directly toward the north.

Once Fitzsimmons was within hearing distance of the camp, he dismounted and snuck in another few feet. He pulled the call from his pocket and stroked the paddle shaped top against the inside of the box. He covered a laugh and stroked the box again. "That ought to get his attention."

Travis turned his head toward the north, recognized the sound as a feeble attempt as calling turkeys. He laughed under his breath. *He's probably never heard a* real *turkey.* He stood and stretched. "Think I'll go take a leak. Back in a bit."

Big Joe stood and flung his coffee grounds toward the fire. He turned abruptly toward the south and pointed. "Sounds like horses comin' this way."

Sheriff White had heard the turkey call, and soon had his posse surround the camp before the gang could react.

Big Joe tensed his muscle and stood tall. "What's the cause of this, Sheriff? We ain't done nothing but sleep and have a bit of coffee."

"Then you don't have cause not to come to town and answer a few questions."

Captain Fitzsimmons rode into camp from the north and surveyed the lot of them. "Already got your boy." He pointed to Travis who was draped over the horse he was leading. "He won't talk, but I know if you've been up to no good, then he's been right along with you. Never figured him to turn bad, but he didn't have the best upbringing."

Big Joe feigned innocence. "It was all the kid's idea. Hell, we didn't know what he was up to until yesterday. We thought he had a claim and we was helpin' him get his ore to the stamp. When we found out he was dealin' from the bottom, we was gonna bring him in. Get shut of him and be done." Big Joe put his hands in the air. "Honest, Sheriff. Honest to God, we didn't know."

Fitzsimmons helped the sheriff tie the rest of the men to their horses. "Take them on in, Sheriff. I'll put out this fire, then be along with the kid."

Travis waited until the Sheriff had the gang out of sight, then jingled his cuffs. "Take me in and get it over with. Damn cuffs are diggin' in and hangin' over this saddle has my guts all tight. Let me sit up."

Robert helped Travis to a sitting position as he spoke. "We have one stop to make before I hand you over."

Travis watched as Robert smoothed the mud on top of the mound of ore. "Better get rid of these clues if you don't want someone seeing them and telling Big Joe you're on my side." Robert laughed and looked at the darkening sky, then back to Travis. "I just can't believe some of the things you come up with. Melons in your shirt?"

Travis grinned and stuck out his chest. The cuffs on his wrists clinked as he pretended to adjust a corset. "I could have stopped a train with them melons."

With Big Joe, his gang, along with Travis, secured behind bars, Sheriff White started asking questions.

Everyone in Big Joe's gang pointed to Travis and all answered in unison. "He's the cause of all this. We're innocent!"

Sheriff White turned to Captain Fitzsimmons. "Gotta let 'em go, Captain. All but your boy. Seems they got hornswoggled by him. Can't prove any different." White opened the cell doors and let everyone go, except for Travis. "Sorry, kid. Gotta hold you until the trial."

Beneath a blackening sky, Big Joe Wilder and crew quickly mounted and rode out of town.

Captain Fitzsimmons stood on the porch and watched them ride north until they were out of sight. "Okay, Sheriff. Let Travis go and follow me.

"Let him go? Are you crazy? He's under arrest for salting mines. That carries a heavy fine and jail time."

"You need to let him go and follow me."

White shook his head as he turned the key in the jail cell lock. "This better not come back to bite me in the ass. I'll have *you're* badge for this if it does."

White kept a close eye on Travis as they rode north toward Millville. He became suspicious when Travis turned off of the main road a mile or so from where the gang had been captured. "What's goin' on here, Captain."

"You'll see." Robert put a finger to his lips and pointed into the distance, then whispered. "Let's leave the horses here and walk in."

Sheriff White started to protest, but Fitzsimmons whispered, "Just follow me, be quiet and don't let on about what you see. Once you see what I have to show you, we'll retrieve our horses and find out what they're up to."

Sheriff White huffed, but did as asked.

They crept through the scrub oak and grasses for a few hundred yards, then Fitzsimmons stopped them, gestured for White to come up beside him. Robert pointed and watched as recognition came to White.

Big Joe Wilder threw the cross aside and cursed as he helped his crew dig up the ore that had been buried under a mound of sticks and mud. "That kid better keep his mouth shut or else!" He flung his shovel aside. "Damn, got a hunk of hickory in my hand from that damn thing you call a shovel." He pulled out a small knife and proceeded to cut the hickory splinter from his hand. "You fella's get this ore dug and I'll go get the wagon from Harry. We'll figure where to take it once we got it loaded. Maybe Harry will have an idea were to keep it until we get it all used." He held up one palm and looked at the sky. "Damn, if we ain't about to get drenched again."

Back at their mounts, Robert said, "Let's head on in to Millville and set up watch. We'll wait for Wilder to get the wagon back here, load the ore, and catch him while he's handing it over to his accomplice." He turned to Travis. "Who was your man in Millville?"

"Name is Harry Long. Has some worthless holes to sell to greenhorns. Can't miss him. Beard to his waist with three gold coins braided into it. All of the stolen ore is going to him. Not sure where he'll dump it. Didn't stick around to see where he went after he took that load. Figured I'd be had if I didn't get back to camp in a timely manner."

White looked the kid up and down. "So... you were in on this?"

"Yep. Reckon I was, but not with Big Joe Wilder." He glanced toward Robert. "Me and Robert had Big Joe figured from a job he pulled west of Tombstone. We just needed proof and me bein' on the inside seemed to fit the bill. I figure if I took the fall, Big Joe would carry on with his plan, then get out of the territory for a while. I happened on the gang while I was checking on another bounty and figured this would be my best chance to catch him. Just had to hope Robert would get wind of it and help me out."

White shook his head. "I had you figured wrong. Figured you'd finally followed in your father's footsteps. Sorry, about that, Travis." White extended his hand.

Travis accepted the proffered hand. "No hard feelings, Sheriff. Most people have their doubts about my intentions, but I learned more from my mother's Bible lessons than I ever did from my father's lawless ways."

Robert grinned. "You know, if you don't want Big Joe to retaliate against you, Sheriff White is going to have to put you back in that cell and hold you for trial." Robert turned to Sheriff White. "Once we catch Big Joe Wilder, his gang, and Harry Long, we'll give the judge the details to get Travis released."

Travis frowned. "I see a problem. If I'm released, and Wilder gets wind of it, he'll have his revenge, even if he is behind bars. Like I said before, he has influence over a lot of people." Travis grinned from ear to ear and held up one finger. "But I have a plan."

Robert listened to Travis' plan. "That might be the best way to play this."

Sheriff White nodded. "I think I can do that."

Travis looked toward the darkening sky. "I'm going back to my warm cell." Hope you have a slicker with you. It's gonna be a drencher."

Captain Fitzsimmons and Sheriff White mounted and rode north toward Millville. Just as they came into town, the rain started. Fitzsimmons pointed to the right. "Let's head to the livery and watch from the loft. I think we'll have a good view from there. No sense getting soaked to the bone."

Fitzsimmons and White watched as Wilder rode into town on his horse, then fifteen minutes later he rode back, driving a wagon with a couple of blankets in the bottom.

Sheriff White nudged Fitzsimmons. "That's the wagon, all right. Guess we'll stay put until he gets back here with that ore.

They stayed warm and dry for the better part of three hours, and just as the rain ceded, Wilder was back with the wagon, but this time the blankets looked to be stacked to the top of the siderails. Willie, Claude and Smiley weren't far behind.

White stood and Robert put one hand up. "Let's see where they go. Hopefully we can get Harry Long in the process."

Wilder pulled up to a shanty, dismounted and banged on the door. A moment later, a man with a waist length beard peered out, then grabbed Wilder by the shirt sleeve and dragged him in the door. Willie, Claude and Smiley stayed mounted and glanced around to see if anyone was watching.

Inside the shanty, Long scratched his chin and ran his hand down his beard. He squinted. "It's a fair piece from here, but I can ride along and show you the way. You head on out toward them Mormons up there in Saint David. I won't be far behind. I'll catch you, easy. It'll be slow goin' for that loaded wagon."

As Fitzsimmon and White watched, Wilder and his crew headed north. "Give it a minute, Sheriff. I'll bet Long is going to join them. Once he's on their tail, we'll be on his. We'll stay off trail and come in as soon as we see Long catch up to Wilder. Shouldn't take too long. That's a rough trail for a wagon of ore. I doubt many use it when the train is much easier. And why would anyone take ore north, when the stamps are right here?"

White shook his head and chuckled. "You got a point. Just thieves and miscreants would take it north."

Long headed to the back of the shanty, retrieved his mule from the corral out back, and proceeded in the same direction as Wilder and his crew.

Fitzsimmons and White climbed down from the loft, mounted and were just a short distance behind Long.

A few minutes later, Long caught up with Wilder.

Fitzsimmons stopped and gestured for White to do the same. "They're just ahead. I could hear hoofbeats and now I don't. I hear someone talking, so they must be discussing the ore and where it's going. I think we should ride in hard with weapons ready."

White nodded. "Agreed."

Harry Long, Big Joe and crew, tried to run, but one shot in the air from White's rifle, bought them to a halt. Hands in the air, they were soon rounded up, handcuffed and back in a jail cell, alongside the cell holding Travis Cooper. Travis winked at Big Joe, but said nothing.

Robert slapped White on the back. "How about a beer?"

White took off his hat, scratched his head and laughed. He looked at the men in the cell and said, "I think I've worked up a thirst. They aren't going anywhere. Let's go to the Oriental."

Travis waited until Robert and White were gone, then stood near his cell door. "Don't get too comfortable over there, big Joe. We'll wait a few minutes, and then..." He grinned as he pushed his cell door open. "...I'll get that set of keys on the wall over yonder and let you out. That nit-wit deputy didn't lock me in after he brought my slop bucket back. He won't be around for a bit. He was headed to Nellie's for a big meal." Travis waited a moment, exited his cell, looked out the window to see if there was anyone on the boardwalk, then let Wilder and his gang out of their cell. "All right, let's get out of here. Probably best if we head in different directions. Your horses are probably at the livery. If I was you, I'd head toward Bisbee. They'll figure you to stick to the familiar, not to the south. Now me, I'm gonna get that girl of mine to keep me comfortable for a bit. I'll let her keep me fed and watered until the heat's off me and someone else has a bounty on their head." Travis started to leave, then turned back to Big Joe, deadly sincerity on his face. "Don't come lookin' for me, or the next cross I plant will be over your dead body."

Travis opened the jail house door, peered out, then strode toward the alley to the north. Big Joe and his gang took the alley to the south and headed toward the livery, glad to be away from Travis and his threats. "Come on boys, let's get shut of this town and that kid. We'll head toward Bisbee and get across the border for a spell."

Big Joe was laughing when he walked into the livery, but his gaiety didn't last. White was in the first stall on the right grooming his horse and Fitzsimmons was in the stall on the other side, leaning against a post, revolver at the ready. White laughed as he unholstered his revolver. "Hey, Robert, look what we got here. How the hell did you get yourself outta that cell?" He scratched his chin. "I bet it was the deputy of mine. Left the door unlocked again, didn't he?"

"It was the kid. He somehow got out, grabbed the keys and unlocked our cell. Before we knew it, he had a gun on us and told us to get the hell outta town and never come back." Wilder shook his head. "Said if we came lookin' for him, he'd shoot us deader than dead." A look of surprise covered his face. "Never took the kid to be a killer. Wouldn't have took up with him if I'd knowed that. Thievin' is one thing..." He shook his head again. "...but killin' just ain't right."

Fitzsimmons nodded. "I hope like hell you left that kid locked in. If he's gone bad, it'll be really bad for anybody who crosses him." Fitzsimmons sighed. "I never took him to be a thief, much less a killer, but I guess I had him figured wrong, too." He looked at White. "Well, we better get these guys behind bars and see if the kid is still locked up." He looked back to Big Joe. "If he's escaped, as you say, Yuma will be the safest place for you for a good long while. He has skills and a good head for how to get things done, and your undoing will be first on his list."

With voice trembling, Big Joe said, "I seen the look on the kid's face. I don't wanna cross paths with him again. I guess the boys and me will take our licks and be done with it. I don't want no truck with that kid. I just hope he knows that."

Fitzsimmons nodded. "I'll see word gets around to that effect. If I ever cross his path, I'll tell him, in person, *while* I'm putting the cuffs on him."

Outside, White shook his head and laughed. "So, you and Cooper hornswoggled a hornswoggler." He took off his hat and ran his fingers through his thinning hair, then looked at Robert. "You should pin a ranger star on that kid... unless you think he's hornswoggling you." He checked the expression on Robert's face. "No. I can see you trust him. So why don't you make an *honest-to-God* ranger out of him?"

Robert chuckled. "I'd never approve of one of my rangers wearing a corset. Much less a corset stuffed with coyote melons." Robert shook his head. "Nope. I think I'll leave Travis just as he is."

A Bad Omen

A Travis Cooper Tale

Arizona Ranger Captain Robert Fitzsimmons paced.

Sheriff McLeod, noting Robert's unsettled demeanor, worked to lighten his mood. He moved to get in front of Robert and put his hands up to stop his pacing. "I'm sure he's just fine. If he said he'd be here, then I'm sure he will be. Just give him a little time."

Robert looked him in the eye. "He's never been late. Not once." He moved past McLeod and resumed pacing.

McLeod watched him for a moment, his eye recording every movement Robert made: Fists open and closed. Brow furrowed. Robert removed his hat. He wiped his brow with his shirt sleeve. McLeod stopped him once more. "You're really worried about him, aren't you?"

"He's never late. More than three years we've had each other's backs, and he's never been late." He put his hat on his head and paced to the jail house window to check on his men. "And he wouldn't ask for more men if this wasn't a dangerous bounty." He turned to McLeod. "Did he tell you anything. Anything at all?"

"Never knew he was comin' until you showed." McLeod scratched his chin. "Did he tell you who he was after? Or where?"

Robert shook his head. With hands on hips, he let out a heavy breath. He shook his head again. "I'm going after him. His telegram came from Charleston. I'll start there." He started for the door, then turned back. "Get word to me if you hear anything." Again, he started for the door and once more turned back. "Send word everywhere you can. Any way you can think to get it to me."

McLeod followed Robert out the door, nodded to the two other rangers waiting patiently, and watched as Robert mounted and hightailed it south, toward Charleston.

Privates Logan Wiles and Thomas Johns, trying to keep pace with their captain, leaned low against their saddles and spurred. Fitzsimmons never let up until he reached Contention. He rode the main street to see if he could spy Travis Cooper's horse. Abruptly, he stopped. Recognizing another horse, crestfallen, he shook his head. "Damn."

Leather creaked as Robert turned in his saddle. Wiles and Johns came to a halt on either side of him. Robert nodded toward the livery. "I'm going to ask a few questions. Move to the front of the hotel and keep an eye out for Bandy Scott." He pointed to a red roan tied outside the saloon. "That's his horse."

"No, sir. I haven't seen Travis, or his horse." He checked Robert's expression. "You're wound a bit tight. You think he's in trouble?"

"How long has Bandy Scott been in town?"

Ben Hopkins, the blacksmith, ran his hand over his bald head. "Oh, I'd say two days, at best. Been in the saloon for much of that." He pointed to one of the many tents. "They might have a better idea than me. He eats in there, most times." He shook his head. "Not often, but at least once a day." Ben put his hands on his hips. "So. You think Travis done gone and got himself in a fix?"

"Get word to me in Charleston if you hear anything."

"Will do, Captain. Will do."

Robert rode to the front of the hotel. Wiles and Johns, deep in conversation, didn't notice him. Robert, not wanting to gain attention from other than his men, moved up and lightly quirted Wiles' horse. Wiles turned, and seeing Robert, kicked Johns in the leg and nodded toward Robert. Robert nodded toward the south end of town. "Try to keep up, this time."

About halfway to Charleston, Robert stopped on the San Pedro. "Cool their feet and let them drink. I'm going on into Charleston. Come on once those horses get a break. Don't come in hard, just amble like it's a nice day for a picnic. Meet me behind the livery."

In Charleston, Robert rode directly to the livery, but didn't dismount. "Hey, Howard. Have you seen Travis about?"

Howard looked up from the water trough he was filling. "Saw him a day or so ago. Said he was headin' to Benson to meet up with you."

"Did he say why or who he might be scouting?"

"Said he heard Bandy Scott come over from Steins. Said he heard Scott was teamin' up with his brothers to make a withdrawal." Howard pointed. "Bandy come through here about two days past. Haven't see the rest of the boys." Howard shook his head. "Travis didn't say where he heard it."

Robert nodded, and pointed toward the back of the livery. "I'll be back there."

Robert dismounted, and once again began to pace. He looked up when a cloud of dust swirled around him, ushering in his men. "Johns, pocket that badge and nose around the saloons. See what the gossip has to offer. Bandy is calling in his brothers to help with a heist. If Travis got in his way..." Robert turned away from them, sighed and turned back. "Wiles, check the tents. See if any of the Scott brothers are around or been around in the last day or two. I'll be right here."

Wiles started to ride away, but stopped. "Why don't we go back to Contention and get Bandy?"

"If Bandy — or his brothers — has Travis, and knows who he is, he won't give him up. He'll use him for leverage." Robert sighed. "He'll use him... and we won't know if he's dead or alive, or where he is until he's no longer of use. And then..."

Wiles pocketed his badge, turned and rode toward the tents, Johns did the same and rode toward what he knew to be the rowdiest of the saloons, and the best place to start.

Robert paced, thought, and waited. He looked up at the weather vane atop the livery and watched its indecisive movements. "Damn, Trav. Where are you?"

Neighing toward the front of the livery caught his attention. He moved into the livery, peered out from the last stall, and watched the front opening, hoping it was Travis.

Deacan Scott dismounted and laughed. "That oughta teach the whippersnapper a lesson or two."

Will Scott dismounted and shook his head. "I ain't never seen a kid so blamed scared. Wonder who the hell he is and what the hell he was doin' doggin' us like that?"

Robert breathed a sigh of relief. *Is. Will said is. Not was. So, he's still breathing. Now, maybe Wiles or Johns will find out where.*

Johns was belly up to the bar, sipping on a beer and watching in the mirror, when Will and Deacon burst through the batwings, laughing and punching one another. Johns set his beer on the bar and listened. The Scott brothers were now just two patrons away from him at the bar. Will Scott waved at Mel the bartender, and ordered each a whiskey and a beer.

"Go on, Will." Deacon pointed to the bartender. "Ask him. Ask around. Just tell him what he looked like."

Will put his hands to his waist and moved them toward his chest. "Gun belt all hiked up to his middle." He chuckled. "I don't think them long arms of his could reach high enough to pull that pistol." He slapped the bar. "Funny as hell. I'd a plugged him if I thought he was a threat."

Mel, knowing Thomas Johns was a ranger, glanced his way. Johns turned his attention to the mirror, and tipped his head toward the Scott brothers. Mel leaned toward Will and Deacon, knowing what Johns must be after. "I know who your talkin' about." He held one hand to around six feet. "Tall, gangly kid. Wears his gun belt high. And if I've heard correctly, that pistol of his is never loaded." He winked. "Wears it for looks." He grinned. "Problem is, he don't know how it looks."

"Dimwit, is he?" Deacon leaned toward his brother. "Can't see killin' a dimwit. Might be a bad omen."

Will huffed. "There you go with that omen shit, again." Will downed his whiskey. "Maybe you're the dimwit." He turned to his brother. "Ever think about that?"

"Bandy has to decide this one. I don't want killin' a dimwit hangin' over my head." Deacon downed his whiskey. "Better down these beers and head on to Contention. See what kinda plan Bandy come up with on gettin' us a payday."

Johns caught Mel's attention, mouthed the word 'where' and nodded toward the brothers.

Mel took the cue. He grabbed a rag and wiped at a spot on the bar. "Where is our resident dimwit, these days? Haven't seen him around for a spell and just figured he'd fell down a well or choked on a pepper."

Will turned away to leave, but Deacon, liking attention, leaned against the bar. "He's tucked away until Bandy says to let him go. Caught him doggin' us and didn't like the company."

Mel laughed. "Dimwit was probably lost and hoped to follow the two of you to civilization. Where'd you run into him?"

"Down south a ways. Near them mines in them hills west Tombstone." He laughed. "Stashed him in one that was played out. He'll keep 'til Bandy has his say."

Will punched Deacon in the arm and scowled. "Don't be tellin' everybody our business." He grabbed Deacon's arm and pulled him away from the bar. "Let's get goin'. Bandy's gonna wonder what's keepin' us."

Johns pushed his mug to the back of the bar top, nodded to Mel, then ambled out. He stood on the boardwalk, pulled off one boot and pretended to be dumping sand from it. He was putting it back on when Will and Deacon mounted and started toward Contention.

With Will and Deacon out of sight, Johns mounted and rode to the back of the livery.

Robert stopped pacing. "Hear anything useful."

Johns dismounted. "And earful and more. Deacon and Will came in laughing about a dimwit. Mel eyed me and understood the reason for me being there. The kid is in a played out mine somewhere west of Tombstone. They thought he was a dimwit." He laughed. "I guess

Travis knew what was coming, hiked his gun belt and played the idiot."

Robert swung up on his horse. "Go find Wiles and head to Tombstone. I'll be ahead of you. I'll check in with Marshal White and see if we can get a few more men together." He relaxed his shoulders, if just a bit.

Marshall White looked up from his desk. "Hey, there, Robert. Got time for a cup of coffee?" He stood, took a long look at Robert and furrowed his brow. "What's that gloomy look about?"

"Have you seen Travis in the last day or two?"

"Saw him about three days ago. Said he was meetin' you in Benson. Said somethin' about a heist. The Scott brothers." He sighed. "Told him they were in Steins — no need to look this way." He shook his head. "That didn't seem to sway him. What's up?"

"I need six or seven men. Travis might be in one of the played-out mines west of here." He nodded toward the door. "I have two men not far behind, but I need to find Travis as quickly as possible."

"What's he doin' in a mine?"

"Will and Deacon Scott."

White raised his brow. "Humph, guess they're not in Steins." He pointed toward the door. "Go on over to Big Nose and the Oriental. See who you can round up and I'll vouch for the good ones." Marshal White started for the gun rack. "I'll pass out a couple rifles." He grabbed a rifle from the rack. "You think Bandy is with them?"

"Bandy is in Contention. Will and Deacon must be heading that way. We'll find Travis, find out what he knows, then he and I, along with my men, will head where needed and hope to get there in time to interrupt Bandy Scott's payday."

Captain Fitzsimmons led five volunteers into the marshal's office. McLeod looked them over. "Well, Robert, you got lucky. We'll take all of them." He handed a rifle and a box of ammo to one of the volunteers, then tucked another rifle under his own arm. "Let's head out."

Robert put up his hand. "You hand that rifle to someone else, Marshal. We don't know where the Scott brothers plan to hit, or when. You better stay put and have a couple men watch the bank, just in case. Send a few telegrams and alert the nearby banks."

Marshal White nodded. "You make a good point. I'll stick here and get the word out, far and wide. If we're lucky, maybe those Scotts will get a train ride to Yuma."

"With Travis in the middle of this, I'm not going to rely on luck." He pointed to the volunteers and his two men. "I'm going to rely on myself and these men."

Eight men mounted, and with Captain Robert Fitzsimmons in the lead, they headed west, toward the hills of Tombstone.

Robert peered up at the clear blue sky, tipped his hat back and wiped sweat from his forehead. *Kid's gotta be thirsty... and hungry. Hope he hangs in.* Robert reined in his horse and the men gathered around him.

Private Johns took a drink from his canteen and wiped his mouth on his shirtsleeve. "What are you thinking, Captain? Splittin' up?"

Robert nodded. "You take two men and check mines to the south. One round in the air if you find him."

"You got it, Captain." Johns pointed to two of the volunteers. "Either one of you know anything about any of these mines?"

Claude, a volunteer, nodded. "Been in a few."

"Know which ones are played out?"

"Two the way we're headed. We'll go there first."

Robert gestured. "Wiles. Take two men and keep going west."

"Sure thing, Captain."

Robert eyed the last man. "Mike, that's your name, right?"

"Yes, sir."

"Know anything about these mines?"

"Not near as much as Claude, but I know my way around these hills."

"Your opinion?"

Mike pointed a bit to the north of where the Captain had stopped. "There's a played out mine just north of the wagon road. I'll take you there."

Robert followed Mike for almost a mile before Mike stopped and pointed to the pilings on the side of the hill. "That there mine is played out. Wasn't much to begin with." He wiped sweat from his brow, then ran his damp hand across his thigh.

Robert and Mike had the entrance of the mine in view.

Robert spurred his horse. "Let's check it out."

Robert was almost to the entrance of the mine when a shot rang out. It echoed in the hills. Robert turned toward where the sound had originated, nodded to Mike, and spurred his horse toward the southeast. Less than a second or two later, another shot rang out.

Why two shots? Robert stopped and listened. He turned his head. He listened. He checked his surroundings and listened. "Those shots came from Tombstone." Once again, he spurred his horse to the entrance of the mine.

Robert jumped down from his horse and raced to the mine. He peered in. *Damn.*

Travis, unmoving, lay on the floor of the cave. Face down. Hogtied.

Robert moved in slowly. He put his hand on Travis' neck to see if there was a pulse.

Travis jerked and sprung to life. Rolling from side to side. His voice was weak but effective. "Get off me! Get off me you blood suckers!"

Robert stepped back as reality came to Travis. Travis peered up at Robert and through a weak grin, asked, "Got any water? I'm a bit parched."

Robert checked their surroundings and noted the bats hanging from the ceiling. "Have they been a bother?"

"Not as bad as the spiders. Cut me loose. We gotta get to Benson."

Robert grabbed his knife from its scabbard, cut the ropes at Travis's hands and feet and helped him to a sitting position. "Why Benson?"

"The Scotts." Travis put his hand to his throat. "Water?"

Mike had been standing at the mine entrance with a canteen in hand. He passed it to Robert. Travis rubbed his wrist where the bindings had been. Look up at Mike and nodded. Robert handed him the canteen. "Go easy."

Travis took a gulp, swallowed, took another and swished it around in his mouth before spitting it out. He took another gulp then poured a bit on his head as he pointed to his hat laying in the shadows. "Get me out of here and let's ride."

"Where's your horse?"

"They hobbled him at their campsite. Plenty of grass and water. Fared better than me, I suppose."

"How about your gun?"

"They hung it on my saddle horn."

Robert turned to Mike. "Ride south and gather the men as best you can. I don't think a shot is going to do it. Then hightail it to town. Tell White to get a telegram to Benson warning them about the Scotts."

Mike tipped his hat. "Will do."

Mike was already out of site beyond the hills by the time Robert got Travis to his horse. "You sure you can ride?"

"Got any food? Kinda lean eatin' the last couple of days, but I can make it to Benson by morning on a biscuit or two if you got any to spare."

Robert reached into one of his saddlebags. "Here's some jerky and biscuits. I figured you might be hungry... if you were still breathing."

Travis shoved a biscuit into his mouth, grabbed the canteen from his saddle and downed a few swallows. He mounted. "Let's ride." He spurred his horse toward the northeast.

Travis and Robert stopped and rested for an hour, just north of Contention. They rode into Benson just before sunrise. Sheriff McLeod met them on the boardwalk. He shook his head. "Hide nor hair. You sure they were headed this way?"

Travis dismounted and offered his hand. McLeod accepted his proffered hand as Travis spoke. "I dogged them for two days. They had settled for a rest and I figured to do the same. I crept into a copse of desert willow. Would have been clear of them if I hadn't spooked five doe. Took off and ran past me, away from the Scotts." Travis shook his head. "Didn't see the buck – but he must have spied me. Took off in the other direction and spooked my horse. Horse ran right through their camp. Needless to say, they were on me in a heartbeat." Travis put his hands on his hips, shook his head and laughed. He reached down, grabbed his gun belt, hiked it to his waist, pushed his hat way off his brow and donned a toothy grin. "I let the idiot do the explaining." He readjusted his hat and gun-belt. "I think they would have killed me if they hadn't thought me an idiot. The one kept mumbling something about omens." He smiled. "I have a plan."

Robert shook his head and chuckled. "All right. Let's hear it."

Robert and McLeod listened, put in their two-cents-worth, and nodded when Travis included their two cents.

At the bank, Travis checked the swing of the front door, then took his position and waited. Robert and McLeod escorted the manager and teller to the back office. McLeod remained in the back and Robert took his positions in the tellers cage. McLeod's deputy, Cole Martin, sat on a bench just outside the door to warn patrons to stay clear until things had been sorted.

Three hours passed before the manager began to question McLeod about the information he'd received that had led to this hijacking of his business. Just as he did, the deputy knocked on the wall. The three inside the lobby readied themselves. Deputy Martin stood, stretched, and strode down the boardwalk, leaving the bank seemingly unattended.

In the back room, rubbing his hand on his head and shaking from head to toe, the manager fainted when the front door creaked as it swung opened. The teller looked down at the prostrate manager. His eyes grew wide as he stood with his back against the far wall.

Bandy Scott laughed as he glanced around the lobby. "Looks a little *lean* for business in here today, boys." He drew his gun. "Now, you at the register. If you don't want me to plug you, empty that cash it into one of them money sacks you got back there and hand it to one of my boys. Deacon." He turned toward his brothers, gun pointed away from Robert. "Get up here and take that bag."

From behind the open front door, Travis slammed it shut and trained his aim on Bandy. When the Scotts turned toward the front, Deacon and Will, shuffled back a step or two and both fumbled for their weapons. Robert had his revolver pointed at Deacon, and McLeod, rifle in hand, strode from the back office, worked the lever and aimed at Will.

Travis, gun cocked and ready, smiled. "Howdy, boys. I've heard it's a bad omen to mistreat a dimwit. Recognize me?" He noted Deacon's dim expression. "Maybe not, huh?" Still aiming true at Bandy, with his free hand he hiked his gun belt to above his waist, tipped his hat back from his forehead and donned a toothy grin. "How 'bout now?"

He nodded toward Robert and McLeod, then back to the Scott brothers. "I see a bit of recognition has come over you, but you boys don't look ready for a fight. Maybe *I'm* your bad omen."

Bandy, eyes narrowed and nostrils flared, was starting to holster his pistol. He hesitated.

McLeod put a round into the ceiling, and in a split second was cocked and aiming the rifle at Bandy. 'Now, you might want to kill that kid, but right now it's just armed robbery. You step it up to murder and you'll swing — if we don't cut you down right here and now. What'll it be?"

Bandy — gun still partially out of his holster — shoved it home and snorted.

Robert and McLeod disarmed the Scott brothers and escorted them to the jail.

Deputy Martin tended to the embarrassed bank manager and teller, then assured all passersby that the bank had reopened.

Travis headed to Café Bonita and ordered five eggs, a slice of ham, a ribeye, biscuits and gravy, flapjacks and a pitcher of water."

The waiter, with brows raised, peered over his glasses. "You got a hollow leg you gotta fill?"

Travis grinned. “Been mining for a few days.”
“Find anything?”
“The bottom of my stomach and *two* hollow legs.”

The Only Ace that Counts

A Travis Cooper Tale

Travis Cooper considered the outcome of working alone, and remember how that had worked out for him in the past. So he waited until morning, then rode back into Cascabel and posted a card to Arizona Ranger Captain Robert Fitzsimmons. It consisted of two words plus his initials. *Jim Corbin, TC.* "How long for a turn around?"

"Oh, should be within a week." The postmaster looked at the inscription on the postcard. He tipped his head to one side and eyed Travis. "You in a hurry, Son?"

"Well, faster would be better."

"The telegrapher is just across the street. Maybe that's the best bet."

"Nope. And I'd appreciate a little discretion with this."

"You got worries about that man?"

"I've got more than worries..." He pointed to the card in the postmaster's hand. "...and Robert will know what they are."

The postmaster stamped the postcard. "Name sounds familiar, but I don't know him... and I wouldn't share this with anyone if I did."

"How does it get handled?"

With the postcard in hand, he held up a bag. "Goes in this bag with these other letters and cards. Doesn't get opened until it gets to Bisbee. Any worries with anyone down that way?"

"Shouldn't be a problem."

The postmaster dropped the postcard in the bag. "You stickin' around for an answer?"

"I'll be by in a couple days. Thank you."

He nodded. "Just doing my job, Son."

Three days later, Captain Fitzsimmons strode into his office in Bisbee, spied the pile of postcards and letters on his desk, and took a seat.

He thumbed through, looking for the most urgent messages. One card from Tucson caught his attention. *Needed. Rustlers. Cocoraque Butte.* He set it aside to check the other correspondence. *Cascabel postmark? What's going on up there?* He flipped the card over and read. He shook his head. "Damn, Trav. I have to head about twenty-five miles west of Tucson." He stood, removed his hat and ran his fingers through his clean, well-groomed hair. *I have to wonder if this has anything to do with his uncle.* He put his hat back on and went to the ranger's bunkhouse.

"Private Johns."

Thomas Johns rose from his bunk. "Yes, sir, Captain."

I need you to go to Cascabel. Take Wiles with you. Travis is going to need help."

Johns grabbed his hat, turned to Robert and grinned. "Don't think he's gone and got captured again, do you?"

"Not yet, or he wouldn't have been able to send me a postcard."

"Who's he after now?"

"Jim Corbin. Gamber, thief, and possibly a murderer. The last was never proven, but maybe that's where Travis comes in."

"I'll get Wiles and round up some provisions. Should be on the trail in about an hour."

"He'll be looking for me, and I can't get word to him fast enough to let him know it will be you and Wiles. But, I'm sure he'll find you."

"Sure thing, Captain. We'll send word if there's a problem."

"I know a postcard takes more time, but there must be a problem with the telegrapher or Travis would have sent a telegram."

"Sure thing, Captain. A postcard it is."

Robert took a seat behind his desk and thought about the postcard from Travis. He scowled and drummed his fingers on the desktop. *Humph, maybe the telegrapher is working with Corbin. Well, I better get supplied and round up two men and get to Tucson.*

"Jessup, Yates. We're taking the train to Tucson. Provisions for a week." Robert sighed. "Make that two weeks. We might get sidetracked to Cascabel once we're back in Benson."

Wiles and Johns boarded the train in Bisbee right along with Fitzsimmons, Jessup and Yates. In Benson, Wiles and Johns deboarded, retrieved their horses and provisions and took the road to Cascabel.

Just as the sun was setting over the Rincons, Johns and Wiles stopped for food and rest by the San Pedro.

Johns spoke through a mouthful of cornbread. "What do think of this Travis kid?"

Wiles swallowed the last of his coffee. "Seems kinda young to be a bounty hunter, but Captain sets store in him, so I guess he's all right."

"You're right about that. I think the kid has a future. Anybody his age that helps bring down the rustlers responsible for his papa's death must have some smarts about him." Johns chuckled. "Sure does look funny in that getup of his." Johns shook his head. "All stupid-lookin' and actin' dumb."

"Seems to work for him. Got him into that camp and fooled Jed Bigler's bunch. That was some good plannin' ,if you ask me. And it got him out of bein' murdered by Bandy Scott's brothers."

Johns lay back on his bedroll, put his hands behind his head and gazed up the first few stars to grace the evening sky. "I guess that's what convinced Captain that the kid had a future in bringin' in a bounty. Kid just has to learn he can't always do it by himself. That couple days in the mine sure taught him a lesson."

Wiles poked at the fire. "What's this trip all about?"

"Seems Travis thinks Jim Corbin is in the area causin' problems. Captain had a word with me while you were gettin' your horse boarded in Bisbee. Said not to trust the telegrapher with any messages. Postcard only."

Wiles threw the fire poker aside and lay back. "I've tapped out a telegram or two. If it's a short message, I can get it done if you can get the telegrapher out of the office for a few minutes."

"We'll work toward that if necessary. Better get some shuteye, Wiles. We still got a ways to go, and Captain wants us in Cascabel before noon."

In Tucson, Robert and his two men deboarded the train and headed to the hotel for a meal before departing for Cocoraque Butte. Robert ate lean. Jessup and Yates noticed.

Jessup, always the clown, leaned back in his chair. "You on a diet, Captain? Or you worried about gettin' gravy on that clean shirt you're wearin'?" He didn't wait for an answer. He turned to Yates. "Captain prefers to be presentable, unlike your sorry ass."

Yates ignored him. "What's in Cascabel, Captain?"

"Travis."

Jessup chuckled. "Caught again... or seekin' to catch?"

"Seeking Jim Corbin."

"The gambin' thief?" He knitted his brow. "What'd he do now?"

"Don't know. Just know he's got Travis's attention."

Yates took his last biscuit and began sopping up the gravy on his plate. "Ever get him for those murders near Dragoon Springs? You know, where the Butterfield stage used to go through." He took a bite of his biscuit, then wiped his mouth on his sleeve. "Heard it was Corbin. Came up on some wranglers from a ranch over that way. Heard them wranglers must have recognized Corbin and wouldn't let him in their card game. Story is Corbin shot them all for what little they had in their pockets. One lived long enough to make it to the ranch house. Last word out of his mouth sounded like *Corbin*, but nothin' was ever proved."

Jessup, pushed his empty plate toward the middle of the table and chuckled. "Hope Travis lets him in the game." He glanced at his captain and knew his joke had hit a sour note. He backpedaled and spoke with Yates about past successful assignments.

Robert listened, but remained quiet and pondered the connection between Corbin and Travis' uncle. He pushed back from the table. "Let's hit the trail. We won't know who's dealing the cards in Cascabel until we catch whoever's stealing cattle over near Cocoraque Butte."

Just as they rose to leave, the rancher approached. He took off his hat and held it in front of him. "I'm sorry to have you come all this way. Turns out it wasn't rustlers. It was a cougar. Should have known when I only lost one calf at a time. Found a carcass." He shook his head. "A lot of sad things in the world, but a mama cow bawlin' for her young'un is one I just can't handle. Too mournful." He sighed, "I guess I got ahead of myself." He looked Fitzsimmons in the eye. "Can I do anything for you? A drink at the saloon to wash down the dust?"

Fitzsimmons rose and offered his hand. "Thank you, but if everything is taken care of here, we need to get to Cascabel."

Johns and Wiles reached Cascabel just before noon. They checked the local business to see if Travis was around. Not finding him, they rode toward the San Pedro and set up camp.

Johns picked up some sticks and placed them under a desert willow and started to light a fire.

"Hey, Johns, put the wood out here in the open and put some green on there. It'll show more smoke. That should get Travis's attention."

Johns, nodded and chuckled. "Good call. I'm used to hidin' the fact that we're in the area, not showin' off."

Two hours later, Travis spied smoke, came in closer to check the occupants of the camp, then rode in. "Hey, there. Kinda warm for a fire unless you wanna be found. Thanks." He looked around. "Where's Robert?"

Wiles offered his hand. "Had business with rustlers up around Cocoraque Butte. Johns knows more than me."

Johns shook Travis' hand as he explained. "Sounds like the rancher is a friend of the governor. That's all I gathered from what little the captain said. He'd be here if he could." Johns nodded. "That I'm sure of." He sat on a log and poked at the fire. "Coffee should be ready shortly."

Wiles handed out cups, then sat. "What's Corbin been up to that got you on his trail?"

"He's staying in a cabin just north of here. Goes into Cascabel of the evening. Gambles. I haven't seen him cheat, but I'm sure he does. Not a man in this world is *that* lucky." Travis held out his cup. "It's boiling over."

Wiles stood and grabbed a rag. He took the coffee pot from the fire and filled Travis and Johns' cups as well as his own. "So, if you can't prove he's cheating, what have you got on him?" He set the pot aside, took a seat on a log and waited.

"I've got him on the Dragoon Springs murders. Dead to rights, so to speak." He had Johns and Wiles full attention.

Travis took a sip, and set his cup on the ground. He flinched and touched his fingers to his lips. "Gotta cool a bit." He stood and paced for a moment, then turned to Johns and Wiles. "One of the men he was playing against in Cascabel accused him of cheating. He made Corbin empty his pockets, and his sleeves, and his boots. I saw what came out of those boots."

Johns stood and put his hands on his hips. "You got our attention, go on."

"Among other hidden things, Corbin had a knife in his right boot. The men in the game made him leave everything on the table until the game was over." Travis glanced at each of the men. "I got close enough to see the spoils, but not so close as to draw Corbin's attention. I've seen that knife before, and it doesn't belong to Corbin. Neither did that gold watch he produced from his pocket."

Travis took a seat on one of the logs Johns had placed near the fire. He leaned forward with his elbows on his knees. He rubbed his hands together, stood again and paced.

Wiles watched and waited.

Johns watched for a few moments, then threw the dregs from his cup toward the small fire. "What's eatin' at you. You know somethin' about that knife and watch?"

Travis stopped, stared at the fire for a moment, then turned to Johns. "The knife and watch belonged to my uncle, Travis Cornelius Cooper. I'm named after him – except for my middle name. His initials are on the knife. I got just close enough to see them. If I'm right, and I'm pretty sure I am, that watch has an inscription. His father gave one to him and his brother – my father." Travis paced. "My father's was in my mother's possessions when she passed. I keep it in my saddle bag. If the inscription on mine matches the one Corbin carries, then I'd say we have him. Just one more item would clinch the deal. And if Corbin doesn't have it, I know who does. Just don't know why. Yet."

Johns turned to Wiles, then back to Travis. "And what's that?"

It was to be a three hour wait for the train to Benson. Robert led his men to the saloon, order them a beer. "Just one. We've got a long way to go once we get to Benson. I'll be at the sheriff's office.

Deputy Anders was just stepping up on the boardwalk. "Captain Fitzsimmons, what's going on around here that needs your attention?"

Robert explained, then pointed to the office. "Can we have a word?"

"Why, sure. What's this about?"

Once inside, Robert looked around at the handbills, then turned to Deputy Anders. "Do you know anything about the telegrapher up in Cascabel?"

"Can't say as I do. What's the problem?"

"I have a man up there who doesn't trust him. Not sure why, just thought maybe you or the sheriff would know."

"Sheriff should be back in a few minutes. I just came back from rounds." He chuckled. "Nothing much going on around here. Gettin' too hot for trouble."

Robert looked down at the ground, then back to the deputy. "Tell him to send a telegram to Benson if he has any information."

Robert, and his men, boarded the train back to Benson – his mind on Travis. He spoke to Yates as Yates passed to the next bench. "Catch some sleep. We'll get a quick meal in Benson before we head to Cascabel."

Yates eyed the captain, noted the pained look, then took a seat beside Jessup. "Captain's real worried about the kid. Gotta wonder about the connection between Corbin and the kid. Could be the cause."

A few hours later, after a small meal, Travis left Johns and Wiles at camp and rode out toward Cascabel. He checked the saloon and hotel lobby, and with no sign of Corbin, he rode on toward the cabin Corbin had claimed.

He rode in quietly, spied Corbin's horse in the small corral near the cabin, then turned and rode back to camp. A good night's rest was in order.

After an evening meal of canned beans and a bit of bacon, Johns called it a night. Wiles and Travis sat by the fire. Wiles kept rubbing his hands together.

Travis grabbed the coffee pot and poured a cup for each of them. "You wanna talk about it?"

"I was just thinking about my sister. I just worry about her."

"Go on. Tell me about her."

For the better part of an hour, Wiles spoke of his worries about his sister and his decision to become a ranger. He yawned. "I think I'm ready to turn in. Thanks for listening."

The next morning, Travis had Johns and Wiles ride into Cascabel with him. He passed the telegrapher's office, then stopped. "Keep those badges out of sight. Now, Johns, you said Robert was west of Tucson. He'll go through Benson to get back to headquarters or to come here, so here's what I want you to do. Send a telegram to Benson. It goes to RF and only says 'We're having a good time.' Just put my initials.TC."

"If it even gets to him, do you think Captain will understand?"

Travis grinned. "It will get to him and I'm sure he'll understand. And when that's done, join Wiles." He turned his attention to Wiles. "Now, Wiles, go to the saloon and order yourself a beer. Keep an eye out for Corbin." Travis held one hand neck high. "Kinda short." He put his hands out in front of his waist. "Porky." He put a finger to his hat. "He wears a tan bowler with a diamond stick-pin. Can't miss him."

"Sure thing, Trav." He started for the saloon, then turned back. "What's the plan if I spot him?"

"Just watch and listen, but don't call attention to yourself. You either, Johns."

In Benson, the telegrapher sought out Sheriff McLeod. "Not sure what any of this means, but figured you'd know who RF and TC are." He shook his head. "Don't ring a bell."

McLeod read the message, then read it again. He grinned. "I know who sent it and who's to receive it. If Captain Fitzsimmons comes looking for it, send him my way."

The telegrapher tipped his hat. "Sure thing, Sheriff."

Travis checked in with the postmaster. Nothing.

"It's a bit soon for an answer. You want me to send word if I get one?"

"No need. But thank you."

After an hour at the saloon, Johns spied Corbin. Johns and Wiles watched him for two hours before Johns caught Travis' reflection in the mirror. Travis strode up beside him and ordered a beer. He spoke just above a whisper. "Hear or see anything?"

Johns spoke as he watched Travis' reflection. "Agree with you. Can't win that much and not have an ace up your sleeve. Literally."

Travis nodded. "But I've got the only ace that counts. Any trouble with the telegram?"

"Just a nosey telegrapher. Wanted to know who RF and TC were and what they were doing for fun in Cascabel."

"What did you tell him?"

"Told him I was RF and I was sending it to my sister." Johns leaned closer. "He asked how much fun I could afford. Wanted to know if I had enough money for a few hands of poker."

"And?"

"Told him I'd think it over. Told me if interested, meet at eight tomorrow night. He drew me a map."

"Keep it for now. Stay put for about another hour, but watch your consumption." Travis pushed his beer toward Johns and strode out.

Wiles turned and watched as the batwings swung back into place. "What do you think he's after?"

Johns put his elbows on the bar. "Not sure. But we'll find out when we get back to camp."

Travis rode to Corbin's cabin, opened a window and climbed in. He searched the bookshelves, cupboards and under the cot, but didn't find what he was after. Making sure everything was as he'd found it, he started for the window. A floorboard creaked loudly and he stopped. He shifted his weight back and forth. The plank moved. He stepped back, knelt, and with his knife, pried at the plank. It lifted easily.

Deputy Cole Martin came in from rounds. "All peaceful, Sheriff. Got anything you need me to do?"

"Go to the train station. I bet Captain Fitzimmons is on his way here and I need to see him as soon as possible. I'll keep an eye on the street."

"You got it, boss."

Three hours after departing Tucson, Captain Fitzsimmons, along with Privates Yates and Jessup, stepped down from the train. Deputy Cole meet them. "Sheriff needs to see you. Says it's important."

Robert, thinking the worst for Travis, took in a huge breath, let it out slowly, and sighed. "Right behind you."

McLeod offered his hand. "Got a telegram here. I'm sure it's intended for you." He handed the message to Robert. "Travis all right?"

Robert read the message. "Sounds like Johns and Wiles are with him, so I'd say all is well... for now. Travis sent a postcard. Got it just as I was leaving for Tucson. He's on the trail of Jim Corbin."

"The gambler?"

"The gambler who might have had a hand in the murders in Dragoon Springs about seven years ago."

"What would he know about that? He was just a kid?"

"Travis' uncle was one of the men who were murdered. Maybe Travis thinks he can prove it was Corbin." Robert sighed. "Know anything about the telegrapher up in Cascabel?"

"Don't even know his name. Why?"

"Travis doesn't trust him."

"If you're headin' that way, ask around about a man by the name of Teddy Morgan. I sent a telegram, but didn't get a reply. His wife says he headed that way about three weeks ago. Was going to buy some cattle and hire a few men to help with herdin' them back. She expected him back last week. Hasn't heard a word."

Travis reached into the hole that had been dug under the floorboard. He retrieved a small lockbox. "I bet he keeps the key on him." Holding the box, Travis sat on the floor and thought back to the items Corbin was forced to lay on the table. He shook his head. "I'm just not sure, but there might have been a key among the other stuff." He set the box, just as he had found it and repositioned the floorboard. He stood and walked to the window. He looked back. Satisfied that all was in place, he climbed out the window, retrieved his horse and checked the perimeter of the cabin. In a small clearing about fifty yards from the cabin, was a fresh mound of dirt.

At Café Bonita, Robert and his men ordered, ate, had coffee, then headed to Cascabel. They camped the first night near where Johns and Wiles had been. They were in Cascabel well before noon. Badges off, they rode straight through town. Not recognizing any of the horses, they continued to the north. "We'll scout around. See if we can find where they're camped."

About a mile out of Cascabel, they spied a rider coming toward them. Relief covered Robert's face.

Travis rode up beside Robert. "Good to see you. Johns and Wiles said you were west of Tucson."

"The rancher met us in Tucson. He had a cougar, not rustlers. Made a turnaround to find out what kind of trouble you've stirred up."

Travis chuckled. "I'd have done this on my own, but I'm not sure who else will be around when I try to take him down."

"Where is this supposed to happen, and when?"

"Eight o'clock tonight. Corbin is supposedly having a game at his cabin in the woods. Might be a trap for whoever shows."

"And you think you can nail him on the Dragoon Springs murders?"

"Thought it possible a few days ago." Travis tipped his head to one side and grinned. "I'm sure of it now."

"You have a camp nearby?"

"Follow me."

Wiles and Johns stood as Travis, Robert, Yates and Jessup rode into camp. Robert nodded toward the logs around the small fire. "Let's sit and talk this through."

Travis waited until all were seated. "As I told Wiles and Johns, I was in the saloon when Corbin was winning way too big. One of the players demanded that Corbin empty his pockets, sleeves and boots. He complied. I saw what he had."

Robert furrowed his brow. "And it was enough to convict him of murder?"

"That, along with what I've seen under the floorboard in his cabin."

Travis laid out his plan.

At four that afternoon, Johns rode into Cascabel and dismounted in front of the telegrapher's office. He walked in, all smiles. "I think I'm ready for that game. Eight tonight, right?"

The telegrapher nodded, then laughed when Johns was out of earshot. "That makes three, plus Corbin and me. Should be a right profitable night."

At seven-thirty that evening, Travis, Robert, and his four men, rode toward Corbin's cabin. They stopped about a mile out and watched as Johns rode the rest of the way, alone.

At eight-thirty, Robert, Travis, Wiles, Jessup and Yates surrounded the cabin, but just out of sight. Robert donned his badge as did his men. Travis rode up to the cabin, dismounted, walked to the door and knocked, then yelled when the door wasn't opened. "Heard there was a game. Am I too late to get in? Got me a wad here that I'd like to try to double."

A moment later, the telegrapher opened the door, eyed him, and waved him in. "What do you think, Jim? Should we let him play?"

Jim Corbin, a look of shock on his face, jumped up from his seat, knocking his chair backward.

Travis grinned. "Cat got your tongue? Or did you slip with that knife of mine and cut it off? Or maybe if you check the time on my watch you have in your pocket, you'll find out your time is up."

The telegrapher ran out of the door.

Wide-eyed, mouth open, Corbin stepped back and fell over his chair.

Travis walked over and looked down on him. "While you're down there, why don't you get that journal of yours out of that hole under the floor. Show these good people how you keep track of your winnings... and your other means of acquiring money."

Corbin began to crawl for the door. Travis stepped in front of him.

Corbin, still on hands and knees, looked up at Travis and rose to his knees. Trembling his shook his head, his waged a finger at Travis. "You're dead. I shot you." He looked at everyone sitting at the table. "Do you see him? Please, tell me I'm seeing things."

Johns took his badge from his pocket, pined it to his shirt, then stood and grabbed Corbin by the arm. One of the other players grabbed Corbin's other arm and they stood him up.

Wiles caught the telegrapher before he could mount. Yates and Jessup followed Robert to the door of the cabin. Robert assessed the situation and had Yates and Jessup tie Corbin. Travis searched

Corbin's pockets, boots and sleeves and retrieved his uncle's knife and pocket watch. And the key to the lockbox. "Throw him on a horse and get him outta my sight."

Robert spoke with the other two players and were sure they knew nothing of the danger they had been in. "Get on out of here. Stay in Cascabel. I'll find you if I need more answers. You're free to leave day after tomorrow."

Travis took a lantern from the cabin and led Robert to the mound of dirt. "Who do you think this is?"

"I've got fair idea it's a rancher from down Benson way. He came here for cattle and never made it home. McLeod sent a telegram, but now we know why it was never answered. I say, if there is any money in the lockbox, we give it to the widow."

Travis nodded. "And the journal will be evidence."

Back in Cascabel, Robert and Travis, along with the four privates, got a table at the hotel dining room. Robert sat back. "Now, do you want to tell us the whole story?"

Travis put the lockbox and key on the table, then put his head down. A moment passed before he glanced at each of the men. "I'm named after my father's younger brother. When I say younger, I mean really young. He was only about nine years older than me. Papa always said he was glad he named me after my uncle. He said he'd be calling me Travis, anyhow, because I looked so much like him. I knew if Corbin got a good look at me, he'd think he was seeing a ghost. That's why I stayed back and let all of you do most of the work."

Robert leaned forward. "I knew your uncle was one of the men killed at Dragoon Springs, but you never mentioned the rest of this."

"Didn't think it important, unless I could take Corbin down for the murders." Travis pushed the lockbox toward Robert. "Open it. There should be a journal in there."

Robert unlocked the box and held open the lid, he grabbed a large stack of bills and laid it on the table, then peered at what had been hidden beneath the money. He looked at Travis. "How did you know?"

"Papa used to be honest about how he got his money, if just for a short time. He and Uncle Travis wrangled together. Uncle Travis got Papa a job on that Dragoon Springs ranch. Papa lasted about two months before he found an easier way to make money. He told me tales about a gambler. Said this gambler was always trying to get them to play, but they knew they couldn't beat him. Not playing fair, anyway. Papa also said that the few times they did play him, he later saw Corbin pull a journal out from his coat pocket and write players names in it and how much he took them for. Papa said it was brown leather with lined pages. Papa got close enough to see a few names. He also saw a few names crossed off. I bet if you look in there, you'll see my uncle's name and the names of the three other wranglers that were murdered. And they'll be crossed off." Travis sighed. "And I bet the name of the man under that mound of dirt back at the cabin is in there too."

Robert opened the journal and thumbed through the dated pages. "August 11th, 1897." He looked up at Travis. "The names of the men in Dragoon Springs are in here... crossed off." He turned to the last page. "And the rancher, Teddy Morgan."

Travis sighed. "I know there isn't a bounty on Corbin. Unlike Corbin's way of thinking, money isn't all that matters. This was about justice. This was about retribution. It was a reckoning of sorts. And you can't put a price on any of them."

Number 17: A Badge of Honor

A Travis Cooper Tale

Travis Cooper deboarded the train in Bisbee, retrieved his horse from the stock car and proceeded to the Arizona Ranger headquarters. He didn't recognize the ranger seated in a chair outside their office.

"I'm Travis Cooper. Is Captain Fitzsimmons around?"

"He's still at the doc's. Might be there a day or two."

Travis knitted his brow. "What happened?"

"We were ambushed on the way back from Douglas."

"Anyone killed?"

The ranger sighed. "Wiles. Took one through the back. Never made it to the doc's." He stood and offered his hand. "Captain had me send that telegram. I'm Jimmy Green. Glad you made it. He said to get you to him as soon as you got here."

When Travis entered the doctor's house, Robert was propped up, asleep on a cot, his left shoulder bandaged, and his arm in a sling.

Travis glanced around the room. Johns occupied one of the other cots, his wound not obvious.

The doctor put a finger to his lips and gestured as he walked toward the back room. Travis kept an eye on Robert as he follow.

"Are you Travis Cooper?"

"Yes, Sir. Captain Fitzsimmons sent for me." Travis sympathetically rubbed his left shoulder, and with knitted brow, sighed deeply. "How bad?"

"The captain will be just fine. Just nicked the shoulder. A few stitches. The sling is just to keep him from moving that arm and tearing them open. Can't say the same for Johns. Took one in the belly." He shook his head. "I think I got everything back together, but a belly wound can fester."

"Any fever?"

"It's high, but no hallucinations, so I'm still hoping for the best."

"Can I stay until Robert wakes?

"Sure thing. The missus and I will be in the kitchen."

Travis took a seat beside Robert's cot. He leaned back, crossed his feet in front of him, crossed his hands over his chest and fell asleep. He woke when his chair started to fall backward. He caught himself, but the chair hit the floor. Now standing, he looked down at Robert and frowned. "'Bout time you woke up."

"I've been awake for almost a hour. You snore."

Travis crossed his arms and chuckled. "Your hair is all over the place and your shirt is dirty, not to mention it's on crooked." He put his hands on his hips and furrowed his brow. "Never seen you so untidy. You're slackin' in the presentable department."

"And I can see you're finally growing into those legs of yours. What's it been? Six months?" He knitted his brow and looked at Travis' face. "And what's that on your face? By God, you're growing up all over. Good thing I don't need you in a corset."

Travis rubbed a finger on his upper lip, then smiled. "I don't have the luxury of a barber every day. I actually have to work for my pay." He stood and hiked his gun belt above his waist and smiled. "But I can still play the idiot." He sighed and pointed to Johns. "Doc says he isn't sure about him, and Green says Wiles didn't make it." He put his hands on his hips. "What the hell happened?"

"Rurales — the Mexican version of us. Mostly lawful, but three got turned for the money they could make smuggling any kind of contraband they could get their greedy hands on. We didn't know they were Rurales until Wiles had one of the smugglers on the ground and the man put his hands over his head and said he was Rurales. One of the smugglers fired, hitting Wiles in the back. It went clean through his chest." Robert shook his head. "Dead before he hit the ground. Damn shame — he was a good ranger."

"They all are."

"Yes, you're right." He rubbed his brow. "They all are."

"So how did you and Johns get hit?"

"Rurales — on the right side of the law — showed up. Caught their own traitors, and one of the smugglers. At least three smugglers got away. We were on our way back with Wiles when we were ambushed just this side of Douglas. Green, my man who sent you the telegram, was the only one not hit. He hightailed it back to Douglas, and when no one could locate the doctor — though Douglas is said to have as many doctors as it does saloons — he got a few men to help get us back to Bisbee."

Johns groaned. Travis went to his side and felt his forehead. "I think he's fever's broken."

The doctor agreed with Travis' assessment of Johns and nodded to Robert. "Your man is gonna be just fine. He'll be a while healin'. No chasin' bandits for a while, but he'll be able to handle paperwork in a couple weeks. Maybe sooner." He eyed Robert. "And how are you feelin' today, Captain?"

Robert raised his arm that was in a sling. "Like you have me tied up for no reason. Can you take this off of me?"

"Let me have a look." The doctor removed the sling and bandage. "Looks good. I think a clean bandage on those stiches should be all you need." He stood back. "If I let you out of here without a sling, are you gonna come back tomorrow with these stitches tore out?"

"I'll make Travis do all the heavy lifting."

Travis, hands on hips and tapping one foot, sighed heavily. "So you sent for me just so I could do all your dirty work?"

Robert looked down at his shirt, shook his head, then grinned. "Speaking of dirty, why don't you stay with Johns while I get cleaned up."

Travis sat with Johns while Robert went for a bath and clean clothes. When Robert returned, Johns had regained consciousness.

Robert put his hand on Johns' arm. "How are you feeling?"

Barely above a whisper, Johns trembled as he spoke. "Like I got hit by a train." He grimaced. "What the hell happened?"

"You don't remember?"

Johns shook his head and Robert explained. Johns' eyes teared when he learned that Wiles had been killed.

Robert patted his arm. "You get some rest. I'll check in on you tomorrow."

Robert, now shaven, clean, and hungry, led Travis outside. He stopped by the hitching post and looked over Travis' horse, then took a good look at his rig, and smiled. "You must be doing good as a bounty hunter."

Travis patted his horse on the neck. "Not bad, and I needed a faster horse, more comfortable saddle, and a rifle. Had a few close calls with cowards shooting at me from a distance. Never had to take a long shot, never wanted to. Always seemed to me that rifles were for hunting... and shooting people in the back. Never took to the latter. Never will. But I guess I better be ready for those that do."

Robert nodded and escorted Travis to the Copper Queen for a hot meal and a beer.

Travis stuffed the last of his steak into his mouth. He glanced around the room. "Fancy... and good food." He leaned back, crossed his arms, and narrowed his eyes. "So... why did you send for me?"

"All of my men have a place in this territory where they know where every creek, wash, hill, mountain or rock is, and how to navigate them. Wiles was my man who knew the area around Benson, Pomerene and Saint David. And he could read sign and track anything from an ant to an outlaw." Robert shook his head. "Johns rode with him on most assignments, but Johns doesn't know what Wiles knew. He just followed. And right now he can't follow anybody. I need someone in that area. For this assignment... and maybe others." Robert took a deep breath and put his hand on his left shoulder. "These stitches itch."

"So you brought me here to scratch them for you?"

Robert grinned. "No, but I do have a delicate situation happening up in Benson that needs attention."

"Delicate how?"

"There is a wedding up there in about a week."

"You want me to hang the groom and put him out of his misery?"

Robert chuckled. "I see what your idea of matrimony is." He shook his head. "No. But I do want you to be there. I want you to stop a murderer. His name is Romey Jones. He was engaged to the bride-to-be. She broke it off, moved from Silver City to Benson and took up with a man by the name of Trix Conner. Romey has vowed to kill them both at their wedding."

"And do we know what Romey looks like? Or am I supposed to wait until someone pulls a gun and shots are fired."

Robert chuckled. "See McLeod when you get there. He has a handbill. And there is a bounty. Seems this wouldn't be the first murder Romey has committed. He's just never been convicted."

"And why is that? Friends in high places?"

"He's the son of a senator. His father sent him west to avoid prosecution in Washington."

"So daddy thought the west would tame him?" Travis huffed. "Why does everyone back east think they can avoid a scandal by shipping the scandalous west?"

Robert stood. "Let's go to headquarters. I have some paperwork to do..." He sighed. "...and a funeral to arrange."

The next day, after the eulogy and the burial of Private Logan Wiles, Travis spoke with four of the rangers who had been able to attend. Two knew him only by reputation. Yates and Jessup knew him professionally. They knew him as the kid, the idiot, and a capable bounty hunter – anything he needed to be, to get the job done.

Captain Fitzsimmons led them all from the cemetery to the saloon. He ordered drinks all around. He held his glass high. "Here's to Private Logan Wiles. A good man and a great ranger. May he rest in peace."

Robert and Travis left the other rangers at the saloon, checked in on Johns, then returned to headquarters. Robert pointed to a chair beside his desk. “Have a seat and let’s talk over this assignment I hope you’ll accept.” Robert took his seat behind the desk.

Travis crossed his arms. “There’s more to it than stopping this Romey Jones from committing murder, isn’t there?”

Robert leaned back and sighed deeply. “Let me tell you the rest of the story.” He leaned forward and put his arms — hands clasped — on his desk. He glanced at the top of his desk, sighed, and made eye contact with Travis. “Senator Jones has made a lot of enemies in Washington. He’s against the Arizona Territory ever becoming a state, much less having a legislature. And on top of that, he thinks we — the Arizona Rangers — are ineffective. Our governor, and others, have had many heated arguments with him about statehood and the rangers. He’s laid out all of our accomplishments from our loyalty to our almost four-thousand arrests. Twenty-five percent of which have been for serious felonies. Senator Jones has scoffed at that number saying it’s inflated and that no one can prove to him that we know how to bring criminals to justice.”

“So what does that have to do with me?”

“I think with your ability to read a situation, figure how to fit in...” Robert chuckled. “...whether it takes a boy, and idiot, or someone in a petticoat, you get the job done. I think you can carry out this assignment better than any of my men.” Robert laughed. “I don’t think a petticoat is going to do it this time... unless you visit a barber first.”

Travis smiled. “A wedding, you say?”

Robert sat back and grinned. “You already have a plan, don’t you?”

“Working on it as we speak.”

Robert slid his chair back and opened his desk drawer. “There’s a catch.”

“And what would that be?”

“The governor wants to knock the senator down a peg or two and prove him wrong. He wants....” Robert took something out of the drawer and slid it across the top of his desk. “...an Arizona Ranger to bring Romey Jones down.”

Travis Cooper loaded his horse into the stock car and boarded the train to Benson. He'd laid out his plan, and Robert had approved.

Robert stood on the platform and watched as the train pulled out. *Maybe he'll see being a ranger isn't all that bad.*

Travis pulled the badge from his pocket. He rubbed it on his pants leg to bring out a little shine on the tarnished silver. He put it back in his pocket. "I'll make him proud."

In Benson, Travis checked in with Sheriff McLeod. "Robert filled me in on the bulk of it, but do you have anything to add?"

"Just that I'm glad you're here." He shook his head. "This town doesn't need a killing, much less during a wedding. And killing the bride and groom?" He shook his head again. "Jealousy is one of the seven deadly sins, and we have enough of the other sins here as it is." He looked Travis in the eye. "So, I suppose you have a plan? And you probably want to see a picture of Romey."

Travis booked a room at the hotel, had supper at the Café Bonita, then did a little reconnaissance. He found a suitable place for the wedding, and spoke with the minister. Four days until the wedding and Travis was just about ready. All that was left to do was to speak with the bride and groom about the timing of their ceremony.

The sun had risen over the Dragoons on what would prove to be a busy day. Only McLeod, the bride and groom, the minister, and Travis knew what this day might bring.

At mid-day, as the guests gathered, Travis listened for the train. A telegram had warned him of the imminent arrival of Romey Jones and that the train he had taken was indeed on schedule. It should pull into the station just ten minutes before the ceremony was to begin.

Travis stood where he could see the guests, who were gathered at a small distance, and the path leading from church yard to the train station. He turned from the guests, checked his Peacemaker, turned back and nodded to Sheriff McLeod.

When the train whistle blew, Travis waited ten minutes then gestured for the accordion player to start the wedding march. Just as the music stopped, Romey Jones came into view. He strolled toward the guest as if he were one of them, just arriving a bit late. He worked his way to the right side and moved up slowly.

Travis kept an eye on the bride and groom as well as on Romey. Romey check the crowd behind him, then glanced toward the minister. Seeing no resistance, he pushed his jacket aside, exposing a .22. His hand went for the grip. He drew it from its holster. He aimed at the bride and fired. Guests fled as the bride swayed back and forth, then fell to the ground. Her head rolled toward the minister. In disbelief, Romey's mouth fell open. He stared at the carnage. Realization hit him. He had just murdered a dressmaker's mannequin adorned in a gown befitting a bride. In disbelief he turned his attention to the minister who had thrown open his robes and was now pointing a .45 directly at him.

Travis, robes fluttering in the breeze, stepped forward. "Drop it. Drop it now."

Romey contemplated for just a second, before McLeod's shotgun to his back convinced him otherwise.

Robert met Travis in McLeod's office. "I hear you got it done. Wish I could have been here to see it."

McLeod patted Travis on the back. "The whole town is talkin' about him. The way things went down, I think his solution was the only one. He knew he had to get Romey to shoot before we could arrest him for attempted murder." He grinned. "I already received a response from the governor. He's boarding a train east as we speak. He wants to tell Senator Jones in person. He wants Jones to know that an Arizona Ranger brought the wrath of the law down on his son."

McLeod reached into his desk draw and pulled out an envelope. The governor insisted you receive this bounty, even if you are toting around a ranger's badge."

Travis accepted the envelope. He moved it from one hand to the other for a moment, then spoke. "When we were around the campfire in Cascabel, Wiles had a lot to say. He has a little sister back in Tennessee who has been living with an aunt since their mother passed... but he didn't want to go back to Tennessee. He loved being a ranger and he loved the wildness of the west. His hopes were to move his little sister to Bisbee so he could look after her. I'm not sure if you knew this, but most of his pay went to her."

Robert nodded. "Yes, I did know, and I'll make sure she gets his last month's pay as well."

Travis reached into his pocket and brought out the Arizona Ranger badge he'd carried on this assignment. He looked at it, then at Robert. "There's a 17 on this badge. I know it was the one Wiles wore. I did this assignment with him in mind. I promised myself I'd honor him. Make him proud."

Robert nodded. "And you've done just that."

Travis handed the envelope to Robert. "This envelope goes to Logan's sister, Lorna Wiles..." He held out the five-pointed ball tipped star. "...and I thank you for the honor, but I can't accept this badge... just yet."

A NOTE FROM THE AUTHOR,

I grew up watching westerns with my father. I was enamored by wildness and freedoms of the west. Especially the southwest.

I visited Arizona in the late 1970s and could never get it out of my mind. It was twenty years later when I had finally had enough of the east, packed up everything I owned, and moved to the Tucson area.

Growing up on a farm, I wasn't used to the city life and eventually found my way out to the desert. I'm now in Cochise County, not far from Tombstone.

I have a beautiful view of the Dragoon Mountains. I watch the sun and the moon as they rise above them. I watch the sun and the moon as they disappear behind the Whetstones.

I don't think I could ever leave Arizona. I need my feet in the Sonoran sand, and my head in its clear blue sky.

So many people pass through Arizona and wonder how anyone could live here. All they see is rocks and brown, dry riverbeds and washes. They never see the beauty in the survival of all who inhabit this arid part of the county.

They're blind to beauty in its rarest form. I drink it in.

Now, a bit about one of my subjects for this book – the Arizona Rangers.

I've taken liberties when writing tales of these elite men. To get to know them better, the facts past and present, I ask you to look up this website in particular: https://azrangers.us/history/

Read about their past, but also about the present day Arizona Rangers who are, every one, unpaid volunteers. They are an amazing group of men and women.

If you happen to find yourself in Tombstone, Arizona, please visit their museum. And don't forget to drop a donation in the jar. The Arizona Rangers are an important part of Arizona's past and future. Let's keep the Arizona Rangers organization operating.

Lewis Kirts

ABOUT THE AUTHOR

Lewis Kirts was born in Maryland, where spring smelled like mud and winter was too cold for her comfort. With dairies on the matriarch side of the family, and orchards on the patriarch side, she was raised on peaches and cream.

She credits her love of western movies to her father, and her love of reading to the English teachers of Poolesville High.

Years of working outside in Maryland had her longing for the warmer climate of Arizona.

She now resides in southeastern Arizona, and after thirty years in the Grand Canyon state, she's finally thawing out.

LewisKirtsWesterns@yahoo.com

Books in the Sendero Esperanza series are:
#1 Trail of Hope
#2 Convergence
#3 Firestorm
#4 Backdraft
#5 King's Canyon
#6 Redemption Pass
#7 Continental Divide
#8 Written in Stone
#9 Fireflies & a Cricket

Short Story collections:
Annie Two Faces
Timing is Everything
Beyond the Stars
Travis Cooper – Bounty Hunter

Made in the USA
Middletown, DE
27 October 2023